CROSSROADS

Gene Salvatore

This is a work of fiction. Names, characters, places, and incidents either are the product of the author's imagination or are used fictitiously. Any resemblance to actual persons, living or dead, is entirely coincidental.

CROSSROADS

Table of Contents

Acknowledgment

There are several people I would like to acknowledge for helping me bring this story to life.

The cover photo could not have happened without the help of Slatington Airport's owner, friend, and pilot, Roger Sell. Thanks for the numerous passes you made in your Piper Cub.

And a special thank you to Roger's granddaughter Reagan for being a lovely and patient cover model.

I must thank Bill Lokes, our longtime Young Eagles Coordinator, and advisor on this book. Bill's eye for detail kept me on track.

And to my editor Carolyn Haley for her expertise and patience. Her editorial assessment, editing, and continuing support have given me the confidence to bring this story to you. That by chance, I found an editor who belongs to the same national aviation organization still amazes me.

Thank you, Carolyn!

Chapter 1: Trouble

Streetlights were just coming to life as the last slivers of daylight cut red swatches through the southern California sky. Fifteen-year-old Kate Wilson looked up toward the growing sound coming from above as she shifted her long auburn hair to one side. Sitting next to her, Jessica Hall, Kate's friend and confidante, also looked skyward from the bench in front of their six-story apartment complex, searching for the source of the sound as it bounced off nearby buildings.

"There!" Kate's hand shot up, pointing to a beautiful biplane passing low overhead, its blue body and yellow wings sparkling against the pink sky.

"It's so loud!" Jess shouted over the deep growl of the radial engine assaulting the evening calm. Both girls watched in awe as the vintage aircraft banked to the left and disappeared, its throaty engine noise drifting away with the breeze.

Kate looked at Jess. "Wow, could you imagine...?"

Jess just shook her head, looked at her friend, and continued their conversation. "Kate, he's a loner, a lot of kids think he's into bad stuff."

Kate brought her attention back to earth. "Jess, he's the first boy that's even noticed me this year, it's exciting!"

"That's not true. I'll bet other boys would love to

2

talk to you." Jess looked down. "Did you tell your mom about him?"

"Well, yeah, I tell her everything, she's cool."

Jess brushed the red bangs from her eyes and looked up at her friend. "How cool was she when she found out you cut class?"

Kate hesitated, again regretting her actions. "Yeah, that was a stupid move. She was upset, she couldn't understand why I would do such a thing, but I promised I wouldn't do it again, so we're good."

In fact, things were not good. Kate was having trouble keeping up with her schoolwork, even receiving a failing grade in English. That and the fact she seemed to be making poor decisions lately created a lot of stress for her parents. And then she had met Tony last week, quite unexpectedly, at the top of the school's staircase number five. Kate had heard rumors of kids hiding out on the top landing, which led out to the roof. Cutting class was something Kate had never considered until, while walking up stair five to her English class, her friend Samantha, after looking to see if they were alone, ran right past the third floor and up toward the roof. Not thinking, Kate followed right behind her, her heart beating faster. This was crazy, but she hated English.

To their surprise, another student, a boy in a black leather jacket, was already at the top of the stairs, sitting on the floor, his back against the wall. "Shhhh," he implored while Kate and Samantha caught their breath. As they sat on the floor, Kate surveyed her surroundings. The gray vestibule door that led out onto the roof had dirt and rust around its edges, giving testimony to its lack of use. On the ceiling, a dusty single light fixture was draped in cobwebs. The place was dirty.

Several minutes after the late bell rang, the young man broke the silence, speaking so low he was hard to hear. "Hi, I'm Tony. We have to keep our voices down. If you hear anything, just stop talking."

Kate had noticed Tony a while ago, and although they didn't have any classes together, she liked how he carried himself. He wasn't tall, but his slicked-back dark hair and leather jacket gave off a distinctive *Don't screw with me* aura that others were quick to pick up on. He didn't seem tough to Kate as they hunkered at the top of the stairwell with their butts growing numb on the hard floor. She'd thought Tony to be cute and easy to talk to that day, so the next day, she sat with him at lunch. She found him to be a good listener, and he seemed interested in, or at least entertained by, her plans for the future. Tony sat there shaking his head as Kate talked about traveling to foreign lands as a flight attendant, or travel agent, or maybe working on a cruise ship. But when she pressed him about his own plans, Tony barely answered, offering an unenthusiastic, "Who knows," which Kate found disappointing.

Jess was not thrilled about her friend's recent infatuation. The petite redhead, who had lived in the area her entire life, was quick to size people up, for better or— in Tony's case—for the worst.

The girls stood up from the bench a few minutes after the plane passed and started toward their building, pausing when Kate's phone rang.

Jess knew by the shock on Kate's face that something was wrong. Ending the call, Kate confirmed, "Erin said Tony's in trouble, he's in the park on the next block and needs help!"

She took off in a sprint with Jess close behind, both knowing that the park was not a good place to be after sunset. As they rounded the corner, they could see that something bad was happening. Two boys ran from the park with frightened expressions while another boy, walking away from the park, laughed, shaking his head in scorn. Erin was nowhere to be seen. Kate's first thought as she looked toward the few people gathered by the swings was to run, run home to safety, but her need to help Tony overcame her fear. She didn't have a choice, Tony needed her!

Jess, conversely, was not surprised at all and followed Kate to protect her. It only took seconds for Jess to size up the situation, looking around for gang colors, or others that were hurt. It was safe to be there. Both girls stopped, not seeing Tony or knowing what to do. Kate was frozen in fear and confusion as Jess continued to appraise the situation, until the sound of sirens snapped Kate back to her senses. An older man walking his dog knelt next to something. In the dimming light, the girls realized it was the limp body of a boy on the ground. "Are you all right?" the man asked, then turned him over.

"My God, it's Tony!" Kate screamed, bringing her hands to her mouth. The man moved back and Kate moved closer, to see that Tony's eyes were fixed, his lips blue as his body began to convulse. Someone asked if he was breathing. "Breathing, he has to breathe! Help him!" Kate implored as the severity of the situation started to take hold. Jessica looked behind her, then grabbed Kate by the arm and pulled her hard to the left as two paramedics rushed past. Kate stood motionless, babbling, "What's happening, is he hurt?" She looked at Jess, who seemed more angry than shocked. The paramedics worked fast, making sure Tony's airway was clear and moving him onto a gurney, which they wheeled to the waiting ambulance.

Kate just watched as Tony was put into the ambulance which promptly drove off. Everything had happened so quickly that the two girls just stood there. A few of the boys standing by the swings were talking to the police, who had arrived moments after the ambulance, and were taking notes. Kate could hear most of what was being said, and even though she understood what she was hearing, she couldn't believe it.

Tony had smoked something from a small pipe, and not for the first time. Kate played back every moment she and Tony had spent in the lunchroom together. He'd never said anything about drugs!

How can this be? she thought.

"Kate, it's dark! We have to go!"

"Oh God, my mom's going to—" As the words came out of her lips, Kate looked past Jess to the woman running toward them. It was her mom!

Anna Wilson had been in her kitchen preparing dinner when she heard the ambulance approaching the apartment complex. She knew Kate would be walking through the door any second, and relaxed as the ambulance continued past their block. But the seconds turned into minutes and the ambulance, followed by a police cruiser, sounded like it had stopped a block away at the park. A shock ran through Anna. Kate was still not home! Somehow her daughter was involved in whatever was happening in the park! Anna bolted from the apartment and flew down the three flights of stairs that separated where she was from where she needed to be, and moments later turned the corner into the park.

As if in slow motion, the terrified mother took in everything and everyone around her, the ambulance pulling away, cops, the man, and his dog. Anna's maternal instincts were panicking, her eyes and ears searching for her child, her eyesight so acute that even in the fading light she spotted her daughter as if someone was shining a spotlight on her. The relief that washed over Anna pushed her into a state of near hysteria as she grabbed her daughter, holding her as tight as she could.

"Kate, are you all right? What happened?"

Kate, still trying to comprehend what had happened, burst into tears. "Mom, it's Tony, the boy I told you about from the lunchroom! He was on the ground shaking!"

"Did he fall? Was it a fight?" Anna asked, holding Kate by the shoulders.

"Mom, no, it might have been drugs." Kate did not want to believe the words she had spoken.

"What? *What!*" Anna was shocked to the core as long-forgotten anger born of helplessness stabbed through her heart. Her knees almost buckled before she caught herself. "Were you with him?" the furious woman yelled as she regained her strength.

"No, Mrs. Wilson, we were by our building," Jess offered in defense.

Anna ignored Jess, her eyes cutting into her daughter like a knife, anger contorting her face. "You get upstairs right now, young lady!

"Mom, you don't understand, I wasn't in the park, we were by our building."

"Oh, I understand all right. I want you upstairs now!" Anna shot back.

But Kate, for the first time in her life, did not obey, her hazel eyes staring at her mother in defiance. "No, he's my friend—I want to know what happened to him."

Anna was taken aback by Kate's reaction but knew her daughter was justified in wanting more information. "I want you upstairs now! I'll find out what I can, Kate. The police aren't going to tell you anything anyway. Go up, I'll see what I can find out."

The two girls turned and walked toward their building, looking at the ground. Jess shook her head. "This is bad, Kate, I'm so sorry."

Kate stopped and stared straight ahead, tears running down her face. "I can't believe this, Jess; they took Tony away, and for all I know he could be dead. My mother has never been this mad at me, I've never seen her react like this."

Kate was beyond confused; she was in trouble, even though she hadn't done anything wrong. Not like that would matter, once her father found out she was friends with someone who used drugs.

The two girls entered their lobby. Kate pressed the elevator button as Jess, who lived on the first floor, hugged Kate before going to her apartment.

"Kate, I'm sorry, I was afraid of something like this happening. It's better you found out about him before really getting involved. I'll see you on the bus."

Kate wiped at her tears and gave her friend a half smile as she turned and walked away. Kate forgot about the elevator and walked up the stairs, trying to anticipate how her father would react to what happened. The events in the park and her mother's reaction had shaken Kate. How could things go so wrong? Maybe her father would be more reasonable.

She opened the front door. There at the kitchen counter holding the phone to his ear was her dad, and he wasn't smiling.

Upon seeing the look on her father's face, Kate ran right past him to her room, slamming the door behind her, and throwing herself onto her bed. As she sobbed into her pillow, surrounded by darkness, Kate realized she was lucky to have not met Tony any sooner than she did. But how could she not see what friends had suspected, what did she miss?

Bob Wilson's six-foot-tall slender frame paced back and forth as he listened to his wife explain what had just transpired in the park. He began to understand why Kate had burst through the front door and run to her room. But Bob didn't feel the same alarm as Anna did. He had just arrived home after his twenty-minute drive from the truck depot where he worked as a supervisor, expecting the smell of dinner and the traditional hugs and kisses to greet him, instead of the empty apartment and stove covered with soup, bubbling over.

As he listened, Bob realized how hard this was going to be for his wife, knowing what she had lived through with her brother. Anna came through the door, still talking to him on her cell phone, ending the call and finishing her sentence as she entered the apartment, slamming the door behind her in an act of anger and frustration, and to make a point to the girl in the bedroom.

Kate, face down on her bed, stopped crying when she heard the front door slam. The ten minutes it took Kate's mom to come home from the park had given her time to reflect as she cried. Kate had started having lunch with Tony two days ago and was beginning to have feelings for him, even though he was known to hang out with a rough crowd. Not being aware of Tony's reputation, Kate's mom had promised to tell her husband about her daughter's new friend when the time was right, but now her mother's trust had been broken. Lying in the darkness, Kate rolled over and waited for her parents to come into her room, her thoughts wandering back to happier times, and her summer days playing with the kids on her block in Fremont.

Mountain View Village was such a beautiful neighborhood. The new single-family homes that lined the streets were attractive to families with young children, all searching for the American Dream. It was a happy neighborhood where everyone knew one another, and summers at the town pool felt like a country club. Kate, who was practical about how she dressed, felt just as comfortable in jeans as she did dress up on Sundays, as did her friends who were all about the same age.

Boys and girls got along fine, and Kate loved the adventures the kids thought up to pass the long summer days. Kate and the other girls invented plays and practiced them before the late-afternoon shows they put on. The girls took turns using each other's backyards, setting up lawn furniture as theater seating, and using their dolls as the audience. They even set up a lemonade stand for refreshments. Inevitably the boys found a way to make the girls laugh so hard that the show stopped and everyone ran around chasing one another, laughing their heads off.

Kate remembered the two mountains near her home. One of her fondest memories was the hike she and her father had taken to the top of Mount Allison when she was twelve. Back then, Kate's father had to work two jobs to provide for his family, so it was a rare occasion when she and her dad got to spend an entire afternoon together. The early spring day was crystal clear and her dad, who had promised to take her mountain climbing, was busy getting things into the family car. Kate laughed as he warned her of the treacherous climb to come, and the lions, tigers, and bears that lived on the lofty peak. After Kate's father packed lunch and a set of binoculars, the two explorers buckled up and set off on their great adventure.

Luckily it wasn't much of a climb, as a road went

right to the top. Arriving at the parking lot next to the TV broadcast antenna, Kate and her father began exploring the mountain's west face, following trails and picking wildflowers for her mother. By the time the pair hiked back to the crest, Kate felt as if she had just scaled Mount Everest. After eating lunch at a picnic table, Kate used her dad's binoculars to watch airliners departing and arriving at San Jose Airport several miles to the southwest, mesmerized at how slowly the giant airliners seemed to be moving as they landed, and envying the many places the flight crews got to visit. She was even able to watch one departing jet for a full ten minutes as it headed west, climbing higher and higher as it shrank from view. Kate loved watching planes fly, forever intrigued by the thought of faraway lands.

Taking a break, father and daughter lay in the grass on their backs, talking about everything and anything as they watched puffy cumulus clouds begin to form. Kate would always remember that day with her father as one of her best.

Kate's thoughts turned to her first day of school after having moved because of her father's job, and how intimidating it was to not know anyone. She was quick to find the homeroom designation signs hung on the fence, and found the sign for "Class 9-101," matching the index card her mother received from the school. *I guess we line up in front of the sign, that was easy*, Kate thought. However, the girl standing near Kate was a total wreck, her red hair pulled back, held in place by a small band, her blue eyes darting around, looking for something on the

12

ground, again and again searching her bag.

"Did you lose something?" Kate asked.

Now close to tears, the girl looked up from her bag. "I can't believe it, I lost my index card, and I don't remember what line I'm supposed to get into!"

"Okay, calm down, where's the last place you remember having the card?" Kate offered.

"I don't even know if I had it when I left the house. I remember going into my bag for a band to put my hair up," the girl said as both of them looked for the card near where they were standing.

"Where were you when you went into your bag?"

The girl stopped and thought for a second. "I was over there." She pointed to the far end of the schoolyard. They ran to the spot, and against the fence they found the relieved girl's card. "Wow, thanks for helping me. I'm Jess. I'm so nervous, today is my first day at this school."

"Hey, it's my first day, too! I'm happy we found it, Jess. I'm Kate. I'll bet you wouldn't be the first kid to come to school without that card," Kate said, laughing. The two girls laughed and hugged, then continued talking, and there in the corner of the schoolyard a friendship was born.

Kate's mind returned to the present, and the not-so-smart moves she had made of late. Copying homework, trying a cigarette, skipping class, and now this. Not her best couple of weeks, but her parents didn't understand how hard a time she was having. She hated that she'd been forced to leave all her friends, her homework was taking forever, she couldn't read well, and now the boy she started to like might be using drugs. The situation seemed hopeless, and she had no idea what to do!

So much seemed to have gone wrong in such a short time. As Kate surrendered to the darkness, her thoughts returned to the bench in front of her building, the beautiful sunset, and the sound of the biplane as she drifted off to sleep.

In the kitchen, Bob held his wife in his arms trying to calm her down. Anna's anger had turned to tears, and she began to shake as the adrenaline wore off. "Bob, please do something. Gordon was enough—I can't lose my daughter!"

Bob looked at his wife and wiped her tears away. "I'll go in and find out what's going on."

Anna grabbed his arm. "Wait, it's more important that we give her support right now. She's been through a lot in the past few minutes, we have to give her time to calm down and explain her relationship with this boy. I'm sorry I got mad at her downstairs."

"Okay, hon," Bob agreed as he stopped and turned into the kitchen. "But we need to do something about this, I just don't know what."

Anna dried her face, went over and tapped on Kate's door, then peeked in when she didn't get a reply, to find her daughter fast asleep. Anna softly closed the door as again tears welled up in her eyes.

"She's asleep," Anna said, walking back to her husband.

Bob hugged her. "Well, she can't sleep too long, I'm sure she has homework."

14

Anna looked up at her husband. "Let's give her some time. If she's not awake in an hour, I'll go in. In the meantime, we should eat and try to come up with a game plan."

Anna poured the burned soup down the drain and pulled out some leftovers as Bob set the table. "Look," Anna began, "things are not as bad as they might seem. I mean, I feel sorry for the boy and his parents. I know Kate only started talking with him at lunch a couple of days ago. They haven't had a real chance to be alone, and I'm sure Kate didn't know anything about his involvement with drugs."

"I hope you're right, hon," Bob said as he finished setting the table.

After dinner, Anna sat holding her husband's hand. "Honey, I know I'm overreacting, but I have a right to be scared! She has plenty to do right now, between homework and her swimming. But we need to think about keeping her occupied this summer. I don't want her hanging out at that park!"

The next morning, Anna confessed to Kate that she was only able to find out that the boy was all right.

Kate was frustrated at the lack of information, and hurt from knowing she might not see Tony again. But she assured her mother that if drugs were involved, she would not have any contact with him.

When Jessie's mother found out about what happened in the park, she reacted the only way she knew: grounding Jess and insisting that she no longer hang out at the park. Jess's dad had walked out on her and her mother a year ago. Now, with little financial support, her mother was working long hours. Tired and feeling overwhelmed, Cindy had little time to think about child psychology, and hoped that keeping Jessie out of the park would work for a while. Even though the neighborhood had evolved into a safe community, Cindy had grown up in the area and knew plenty of families destroyed by drug addiction.

"I don't get it, Jess," Kate said. "You had nothing to do with any of this, and you're the one who warned me about Tony."

"Tell me about it! But my mom has a lot on her mind right now. Besides, this is how she always reacts. In a few days, she'll calm down."

Kate admired how well Jess was handling the situation, but still felt terrible after hearing of her friend's punishment. Kate decided that just letting time pass and hanging out with Jess might be the best course of action.

A few days later, word reached a few students that Tony had been using crack cocaine and was released from the hospital to a juvenile rehab center until early July. His parents in the meantime were planning to relocate, hoping to give Tony a fresh start in a new school.

Kate was in the hall changing class when she heard the news, stopping her in her tracks. "How could he be so stupid!" She burst into tears and ran to the ladies' room, not to be seen crying. It was a good ten minutes before she stepped out of the stall to find Jess standing there waiting for her. Jess, not speaking a word, walked over and hugged her friend, tears streaming down their faces.

Chapter 2:
Plans

Although things had settled down at home, Kate's father was preoccupied with the events in the park, determined to assure his wife that Kate was occupied for the summer. Unfortunately, no such plan was forthcoming, until out of desperation he picked up the phone and called his brother Frank.

Frank's wife, Sue Wilson, was standing at the kitchen sink cleaning up from dinner when the phone rang. "Bob, how are you, and how's the family?"

"Great," Bob answered, not wanting to tip his hand. "How are you?"

"Things couldn't be better. Hold on, let me see if Frank's around."

Bob smiled to himself as he waited for Susan to return to the phone, always amazed by how his sister-in-law was always so upbeat and happy. Bob's brother had met Sue back in the 1970s after finishing his tour of duty in the Army. Frank had been a sergeant in an Army recon platoon, serving one tour in Vietnam. Upon leaving the service, he used the money he'd saved to put a down payment on a parcel of land in Napa Valley and began planting grapevines.

He met Susan at the local farm supply when he spilled a bag of fertilizer in front of her cash register. "Well, is it the right color?" Sue asked, not the least bit flustered, then went out of her way to help Frank clean up the mess. Frank became infatuated, and after three consecutive days of buying this and that, he finally got the nerve to ask Susan out.

Susan and Frank were married a year later and together built the vineyard into a well-respected source of grapes for the surrounding wineries.

Frank was built like a bull. His fingers were short and stubby, showing the wear of many years outdoors working the vines. And he always had an answer for any situation, which is why Bob was reaching out to him.

"Hey, buddy, how you doing?" Frank asked, always happy to hear from his younger brother. "How's the family?"

"Well, to tell you the truth, Frank, that's why I'm calling."

Frank and Susan were unable to have children of their own and were very attentive to Kate. They took great pleasure in watching her grow and were apprehensive about how she would fare in the move south. Frank listened to the short version of what had happened in the park. "Well, I'm sure Kate will figure things out."

Bob hesitated for a moment, then continued. "There's another problem. She's not doing that well in school, and her grades are slipping, plus we had a few issues with her. She's active with the swim team and made a few friends, but that's not what worries me. Frank, I'm worried about the summer. I don't think she's going to have enough to keep her occupied. Besides that, Anna is flipping out after what she went through with Gordon."

"I don't think Anna has reason to worry, but all right—we'll use the five problem-solving steps I was taught in the Army."

Bob waited while Frank recited, "For starters, you have to realize there is a problem, and it seems you've already done that. Number two: identify the problem, which sounds like Kate needs something to keep her busy for the summer or she might hang out with the wrong crowd. Number three: come up with several solutions to the problem. Four: choose one of those solutions. And five: implement that solution."

Bob just shook his head. "That's great, Frank, except I don't have any ideas."

"Well, she could join the Girl Scouts. Or how about a summer camp?"

"Frank, we can't afford a summer camp this year."

After a moment of silence, Frank exclaimed, "Bob! What if Kate spends the summer at the vineyard with Susan and me? There's plenty to keep her occupied, and it won't cost you a dime."

"Frank, I couldn't put you out like that."

"Nonsense. Let me speak to your wife and I'll talk her into it. Put her on the phone."

"Anna, Frank wants to talk with you," Bob said, raising his eyebrows to warn Anna.

She took the phone. "Hi, Frank, what are you two gangsters cooking up?"

"Anna, I think I have the perfect solution to your problem."

"I didn't know we had a problem," Anna

responded, spinning around and staring at her husband.

"Look, Anna, Bob just filled me in on what's been going on down at the park. And I know that you're both concerned about this summer. Well, I have an idea for the two of you to consider. Why doesn't Kate spend the summer with us? We'd love to have her, and there's plenty for her to do."

"I don't know, Frank, that's putting you out. Are you sure Sue would go along with something like that?" Anna again looked at her husband, who shrugged and walked away.

"Sue is standing right here listening, she wants to talk to you. Talk it over and the two of you can hash out the details." Frank handed the phone to his wife.

That evening, Anna sat staring at the TV, even though it wasn't on. "What are you thinking about, hon?" Bob asked, looking over his newspaper.

"I think it's a good idea."

"What's a good idea?" Bob put the paper down and looked at his wife.

"I think Katie spending the summer with Frank and Susan is a good idea. I just have the feeling that Kate needs a reset. A chance to figure out why she is acting so differently. I want her to spend some time away from here, from peer pressure, and away from that park."

Anna broke into tears. "I'm sorry, I miss my brother," she whispered, then buried her face in her hands and wept.

Bob sat next to his wife and held her close. "It's going to be all right, honey, you can break it to her tomorrow, let her know it was my decision. I'll be the bad guy; she can blame me."

The next morning, Kate screamed, "Mom, how could you do this without talking to me!" and ran back into her room.

"I'm sorry, dear," Anna called after her, "but your dad has already made up his mind. And Uncle Frank and Aunt Susan will be heartbroken if you say no. Besides, there's nothing for you to do here." With that pronouncement, Kate Wilson's fate was sealed, at least until September.

At lunch the next day, Kate told Jess, who couldn't believe it, either. "Wow, eight weeks of hard labor! I thought I got a raw deal. Do they have running water? You might have to carry it back from the river every day."

Kate smiled, appreciating the humor in this Greek tragedy. "Maybe I'll have to be the scarecrow and stand in the field all day!"

They laughed. "You'll meet a farm boy, and spend the rest of your life stomping grapes with your bare feet like Lucille Ball did on that show," Jess quipped, crossing her eyes for effect, as Kate took a sip of her soda. Kate laughed so hard, the soda came out of her nose, causing both girls to laugh until they couldn't breathe. In the end, the two hugged and headed off to class. Two weeks later, the school year ended with the friends tighter than ever.

The day before departing for Napa, Anna was out picking up a few last-minute items, giving Bob a chance to speak with his daughter alone. Bob found her in the living room and sat on the couch next to Kate, facing her. "Kate,

I think it's important for you to understand why your mother is so upset about what happened to Tony. A few years before you were born, your mom's brother Gordon broke his right leg, hip, and back in a terrible car wreck that put him in the hospital for three months. Even after he was released, he needed strong painkillers just to walk and ended up addicted to them. He lost everything—his job, his girl—and he began suffering from depression. Your mom did everything she could for him, and we tried several times to get him off the drugs. Sweetheart, your uncle died of a drug overdose. And it took years for your mother to get over it. Your coming along finally got her out of her depression. The incident in the park scared the hell out of her. She's been upset ever since. I need you to do this for her."

Kate was shocked. "Mom told me he got sick, but nothing more. How old was he when he died?"

Her father's eyes filled with tears. "Gordon was twenty-three, Kate. Just twenty-three. He was so full of life; funny and ambitious; and it was all taken away from him."

Kate hugged her father and began to understand why her mother was overreacting.

"So do this for your mom, Kate. She's a wreck." Bob wiped a tear from his eye. "And please don't say anything about our talk, at least not yet. Okay?"

Kate gave her dad another hug. "Heck, I didn't have any plans for this summer, anyway."

Bob hugged his daughter. "That's my girl."

The next day, Kate took one last look at her room

22

before she and her parents departed for Napa. The drive took all morning and well into the afternoon, along the I-5 interstate. Kate enjoyed the ride through the hills north of Los Angeles but found most of the ride boring, giving her plenty of time to think. She was eager to see her uncle and aunt, but the thought of spending the entire summer at their vineyard scared her. "Mom, when am I going to see you again?"

"Honey, your father has to work, but we'll be able to talk or text as often as you like."

"What am I going to do there? I mean, are there other kids?"

"Yes, dear, we spoke about that with your aunt and uncle. I know your aunt mentioned a fair, and I'm sure there are plenty of things to do in the area, and she mentioned introducing you to another school student."

"Oh, great!" Kate texted to a group of friends. "My mom just told me I might be hanging out with the farmers. Maybe we can crush grapes together."

Kate watched the landscape change as the weary travelers neared their destination. Farm equipment was everywhere, and grapevines in straight rows of green and brown ran to the horizon. To the east, light-brown rolling hills covered in dried grass and dotted with a random sprinkling of oak trees rose from the valley floor, creating a wall of beauty. Even the air smelled different, cleaner, with a subtle sweetness to it.

Kate's dad had arranged to take the following Monday off so the family could spend the weekend in Napa with Frank and Susan before returning home. The difference was that this time Kate was being left behind.

Bob enjoyed driving, his many years driving tractor-trailers giving him plenty of stamina during the long haul. But he missed being up in the big cabs and the view they afforded, plus his back didn't hurt as it did now.

"We're here," he announced, turning left into his brother's vineyard. Anna looked back from the front seat. "Honey, things are not as bad as you're making them out to be. I'm sure you're going to have a good time," she assured Kate as the car came to a stop.

Not so sure, Kate was at least looking forward to seeing her aunt and uncle. They had a way of making her feel special and had to be the happiest people she knew.

"Here they are!" Frank said as he stepped out of the house, his wife close behind. Frank and Susan had just finished remodeling the entire house, and Frank was eager for his brother to see the finished product.

Bob and Anna stepped out of the car, Bob stretching his back as they admired the work Frank and Susan had done to the house. It was still white, with black shutters on the windows. The wraparound porch rails had just been renovated, and above the porch, the second floor sported two new gables, their windows open to the breeze. Anna loved the fresh landscaping, with its wide variety of shrubbery and colorful flowers, which made the place look brand new. Bob was happy to see that the large live oak on the left side of the house was still there, its ponderous limbs reaching out in all directions, providing shade to most of the house. As Kate got out, the first thing she noticed was the tractor parked where it always was, across from the house, the fresh mud on its tires a testament to its daily use. Kate had always been in awe of the powerful machine and was happy to see it was still around.

"Wow, Frank, they did a beautiful job, it looks great!" Bob complimented as the two brothers hugged. "Thanks, Bob. It took a while!"

"Look at how big you've grown!" Susan exclaimed as she hugged Kate. Anna came around the front of the car and gave her sister-in-law a big hug. "My goodness, Susan, the house looks wonderful!"

"How was the ride, Anna?" Sue asked, adding in a whisper, "and how is Kate doing with all of this?"

"She's good, Sue, and it's so generous of the two of you."

"Nonsense. We'll get to spend some time with our beautiful niece. You have no idea how excited we are, and we have lots of fun things planned."

Susan had prepared a wonderful dinner, and Frank brought out a bottle of wine made with grapes from his vineyard. After dinner, Bob and Frank went out on the back deck to talk, leaving Sue, Anna, and Kate to clean up.

"Frank, I just don't understand what's going on with Kate. Her marks are down, she hates homework, and then this park fiasco."

Frank shook his head. "Did anyone hear about what happened to the boy?"

"He's all right, I gather. Kate heard he's in a youth detox facility, and his parents relocated so he could start a new school in the fall."

"You did say that she had only just met this boy and didn't know him that well. I'm sure it must have shaken her up. How is she doing?"

"A lot better, but she was upset with our decision to bring her here, so yesterday I told her about Gordon and why her mother is so upset. Anna made the final decision to bring her here, but that doesn't stop me from feeling guilty about taking the job in LA"

"You shouldn't feel that way, Bob. You took that job because it was a big step up."

Bob gave his brother a brave smile. "I know, I know. So what kind of things do you have in mind for her this summer?"

"Don't worry," Frank answered with a smile. "We'll keep her busy."

After helping clear the table, Kate stepped out onto the porch and looked up. The sky had turned deep blue, its wispy clouds tinted pink by the setting sun. As she strolled over to the tractor, a soft breeze rustled the leaves of the live oak. Kate turned to look at the tree, her mind wandering between the beauty and peacefulness of the evening and a feeling of despair. This was the first time she would be separated from her parents, and she was scared. Later that evening, after saying goodnight, Kate sat on the bed in the small room at the top of the stairs looking at her aunt's sewing machine. Susan's hobby was sewing quilts depicting storybook characters and donating them to the local children's hospital.

Kate cried into her pillow for a bit, then just lay and listened to the quiet, lulled by the gentle movement of the curtains. Her last thoughts as she drifted off to sleep were about her friends at home, her mom and dad, and being left behind.

Upon waking, Kate heard birds chirping outside and conversation and laughter coming from the kitchen. She sat up and smiled, eager to get downstairs, then it hit her. "I can't believe they're leaving me here!" A short time later, she went down the stairs, dressed and sporting a brave face.

"Good morning, sleepyhead!" greeted her mom, giving her a big hug.

"Good morning, Kate," Sue added, pulling out a chair. "Sit down right over here and let me get you some breakfast, dear."

The men were already at the table. Kate gave them both a kiss before taking her seat.

"I hope you brought your walking shoes, Kate," Anna said, putting juice on the table. "Your aunt said she doesn't mind driving, so have your breakfast and go get ready. We're going to spend the day in San Francisco!"

Kate's face lit up. "San Francisco! Wow! Thanks, Aunt Sue!"

Sue smiled. "Well, your dad is tired of driving, so the two boys are staying home to watch the ball game."

Bob turned and looked at his sister-in-law. "Yes, thanks for the break, Sue. Just don't go falling off any trolley cars."

Only the men laughed at that one.

The women had a great time in San Francisco, visiting all the sites the "City by the Bay" had to offer, and

Kate had no problem that night falling asleep. The next morning began the same as the day before, except for it being the start of Kate being stranded in Napa. At least that's how Kate saw it as she took a seat at the table. A moment later, Bob came in through the screen door in a huff. "Okay, honey, the car is packed and ready to go. Sue, I didn't know Frank slept so late."

Sue couldn't contain her laughter. "Your brother's been working on the spray equipment since 6:30, dear boy. He should be walking in the door any second now."

Kate was surprised. She knew some people started their day early, she just didn't know her uncle was one of them—a revelation that was reinforced when she heard the throaty sound of an engine approaching the house. Spinning around, Kate looked out the window behind her and saw her uncle driving up on the tractor, a cloud of dust drifting behind him on the gentle breeze. Frank brought the big machine to a stop, shut down, and dismounted in one fluid motion. Kate, shifting her gaze to the front window, was amused at the dust that engulfed her uncle without his even noticing. Frank brushed himself off before stepping onto the porch and entered the kitchen grinning from ear to ear.

"Good morning, lazy bones."

Bob rose from his seat and was greeted by his brother with a bear hug. "Good morning, Frank. Is it this beautiful every morning?"

Frank walked over to the sink and kissed Sue before washing his hands. "Yep, just about. We do get some morning fog this time of year, but not for the past two days. I guess our house guest has brought the good weather with her." Frank smiled at Kate. "I hope you realize, young lady, that we start the day early around here," he added with a grin. Kate didn't know if he was kidding or not. "That's okay, Uncle Frank," Kate answered, fudging a smile. "It would be a crime to sleep through such beautiful mornings."

"That's what I like to hear," Frank announced as he took his seat at the table.

After breakfast, Kate helped her aunt clean up while her mom and dad got ready to leave. Anna stopped. "Kate, remember to give your aunt help around the house, and don't be afraid to clean up after yourself."

"Don't worry about a thing," Sue assured Anna. "Kate will have plenty to keep her busy, and I promise you she'll have a great time here"—directing her comment to the girl putting the last dish away. "I ran into Laura Gillman—they own Rosewood Vineyards, her son Bruce is sixteen—anyway, Laura told me she'll let us know if his school has any summer events Kate can attend."

Kate didn't know what to make of that statement. *Great, meet a boy in Napa and have purple feet*, she thought but didn't say.

Before getting into their car, Bob hugged his brother and sister-in-law then walked over and handed his daughter a greeting card. "Try to make this easy for her," he whispered as he gave Kate a kiss and hug before getting into the car. Anna, tears in her eyes, held Kate's hand. "Sweetheart, give it some time. Besides, there's nothing to do at home." That raised the hairs on the back of Kate's neck a little, but all she said was, "I'll be just fine, Mom, it'll be fun."

Anna gave Kate a long hug. "I'm going to miss you so much."

Kate had tears in her eyes as she gave her mom a kiss. "I love you, Mom." And with that, Bob and Anna drove off, leaving their little girl for the first time in their lives.

"Thanks for the help cleaning up, Kate. Why don't you put that card upstairs while I find the keys to the pickup. The two of us are going into town for a few items you're going to need this summer."

"Mom packed a lot of things for me, Aunt Sue, you don't have to buy me anything," Kate replied politely.

"I'm sure she didn't pack what we're shopping for, and I know your parents gave you spending money, but you just put that away. Your uncle and I are paying you a salary while you help out on the vineyard this summer."

"What? Mom didn't tell me I'd be earning money. Thanks!"

Susan laughed and kissed Kate on the forehead. "Okay, go get ready, we need to find you some work boots."

Kate gave her a look before running up the stairs to grab her pocketbook. She took a moment and opened her father's card. The cover featured a painting of a father and young daughter holding hands, walking down a tree-lined dirt road. Kate opened the card, then held it to her heart for a long moment, her eyes filling with tears.

Inside the card, Bob had penned a short message.

Thank you for being brave. Love, Dad XOXO

# # #

Kate sat next to the open truck window lost in thought as the wind blew through her long hair. Approaching Napa Valley's historic commercial hub, St. Helena, Kate wondered if things were the same since the last time she had been there. She got her answer as they drove into the heart of town, where a seven-year-old Kate had always imagined the ornate lampposts as soldiers, standing guard, protecting the century-old buildings from the march of time.

Sue found parking across from Kate's favorite building. The two-story brick building featured steel columns supporting a sage-green balcony. Kate loved the Victorian-style spire dated 1892, embossed with the square and compass of the Freemasons, and topped with a white flagpole.

As she walked with her aunt to the hardware store, Kate couldn't resist giving a passing lamppost a quick pat, thanking the soldier for a job well done. Entering the store, Kate stopped, not knowing where to look first, as a menagerie of tools, hardware, hoses, and farm supplies greeted the pair. Kate followed her aunt past racks of tools, hardware, and cowboy hats. But nothing prepared Kate for the pungent aromas that overtook her senses as she continued toward the coverall and shoe department. The smells of leather, rubber, and fabric that hit Kate would forever be imprinted into her memory.

Susan, oblivious to the bouquet, began picking out things Kate would need for the summer. Besides work

31

boots, Sue found a nice-fitting pair of Carhartt coveralls, work gloves, and a baseball hat. Satisfied that she had everything she came for, Sue proceeded to the register. As Kate watched her aunt check out, it became clear that she would be doing a lot more than taking out the trash and vacuuming rugs this summer.

Frank was driving up from the lower fields just as Kate and Sue got home. Again, Kate watched a cloud of dust follow behind the tractor like a lost puppy and continue past as her uncle shut down. "Well, girls, how did you make out in town?" Frank yelled as he made his usual dismount, paying no attention to the dust that swirled around him.

Funny, Kate thought, *he must do that a lot because he gets off the tractor the same way every time.*

"Well, Uncle Frank," Kate replied with a skeptical look, "I have work boots, gloves, canvas coveralls, and a baseball hat with a tractor on it." Kate lifted one eyebrow, giving her uncle the classic *What the heck did I get myself into?* expression.

"Don't worry, I promise we won't take any pictures of you," Frank assured her. "Go put your new gear on, and come down for lunch. I have work to do this afternoon and could use a hand." He grabbed packages from the back of the pickup as Kate scampered upstairs.

Chapter 3:
The Tractor

Kate was still a bit confused as she inspected her new work boots. They smelled new, with heavy brushed leather high enough to cover her ankles, and thick rubber soles built to protect her feet. The canvas coveralls were another story, their heavy brown fabric, stiff as cardboard, more a suit of armor than work clothes. Kate finally came down for lunch looking like a newly minted farmhand, in her new boots, stiff coveralls, and baseball hat. She hung her work gloves and hat on wall hooks next to her uncle's. "Well, I guess I'm ready for anything," she announced as she took a seat.

"You look just fine, dear," Susan replied as she placed a bowl of salad on the table. Her uncle walked over to Kate, looked at her brand-new work boots, and stepped on Kate's left foot, smudging the clean leather with the bottom of his boot. Kate and Sue looked at him in disbelief, causing Frank to laugh.

"When I was a kid, I came to work with new boots, one guy walked over and stepped on my toe getting my boot dirty. Boy, did I get mad, until one old-timer explained that it was a tradition. You see, honey, now that your boots aren't so pretty, you'll pay attention to what's going on around you instead of trying to keep your shoes clean. These boots are made to get dirty."

Sue came over with a pitcher of lemonade, put it

on the table, and gave her husband a good punch in the arm.

"Ouch! What was that for?" Frank winced, holding his arm.

"That's so you won't have to worry about hurting your arm!" his wife answered sarcastically, as Sue and Kate began laughing.

"Hey, I'm just teaching the kid," Frank said, trying not to smile.

As they ate, Frank laid out the afternoon's mission. "Kate, I'm getting ready to plant grapevines this autumn on a two-acre plot at the bottom of the hill. I've been installing the support trestles to support the vines, and I could use a hand running the irrigation tubing."

"Of course, Uncle Frank, you don't have to ask. I would love to help. Besides, it's such a beautiful day."

"Honey, I'll always ask. Remember, you don't have to do anything you don't want to do, or don't feel safe doing," Frank replied looking at Sue, who nodded in agreement. "Sweetheart, we want you to have fun this summer, learn a few things, and enjoy your time here."

"Thank you, Uncle Frank, it sounds good to me. I'm happy to help," Kate replied, smiling.

As Kate ate lunch, a feeling of warmth washed over her like a wave. She felt mature and respected at the same time. Sue joined them at the table for lunch as Kate took it all in, the beautiful day, the house, and her aunt and uncle. Kate knew she was lucky to have them. After lunch, Kate carried her plate to the sink, then followed her uncle out through the front door.

34

"Don't forget your hat and gloves," her aunt reminded.

Once outside, Kate headed for the pickup but noticed her uncle walking over to the tractor.

"It gets a little muddy down at the bottom of the hill, so we're taking the tractor," Frank told the new farmhand.

"Where am I going to sit?" Kate asked as she inspected the hulking, green piece of farm equipment.

"You're not sitting. Walk around to the back and I'll explain."

Kate came around to the rear of the machine, not knowing what to expect.

"I'm going to sit and you are going to climb up behind me and stand on this flat bar between the rear fenders, and you're going to hold on to the back of the seat." Frank pointed out the cross beam between the tall rear wheels. "We're not going to be driving very fast, but keep your knees bent so you don't get jostled too much. Your legs are your shock absorbers."

Kate was surprised at her uncle's suggestion; heck, she didn't go anywhere without a seat belt. Frank climbed up and sat down on the only seat. "Okay, Kate, come on up."

Kate lifted her right foot onto the bar, then reached forward with her left hand and grabbed onto the back of the seat to pull herself up, appreciating the firm support of her new work boots.

Things sure are different around here, she thought as she climbed up between the two tractor wheels. The enormous tires smelled of rubber and had large V-shaped treads for traction. The mud that was caked on the inside of the fenders and bottom of the tractor testified that things would get messy. Kate felt very grown-up standing on the bar behind her uncle as she took in the vista her lofty perch provided...until her uncle snapped her out of the moment.

"Now watch what I'm going to do, Kate. I'm pushing my right foot down on the brake pedal to hold the tractor where it is, then pushing down on the clutch pedal with my left foot, disconnecting the rear wheels from the engine. Now I can start the tractor without it lurching forward. This long lever coming up from the floor is the shifter." Frank pointed to the black knob on the end of the lever. "Look at the H-pattern printed on the knob. The numbers above and below the H indicate gears, and the shape of the letter shows you how to move the shift lever from one gear to the other. We start in first gear at the upper left, move straight down into second, then up, across, and up into third, and straight down into fourth. I start the engine by turning this key and pressing this button."

"Where's the gas pedal, Uncle Frank?"

"Tractors don't have a gas pedal; they have a throttle, which is this lever sticking out from under the steering wheel like an hour hand pointing at three o clock."

Kate leaned forward to observe where the throttle was located. Frank continued, "Once the engine is running, you move the throttle forward a little to increase the

36

speed of the engine. We are already in first gear so you *slowly* bring your left foot up until you hear the engine labor a bit, then raise your right foot off the brake, lift the left foot slowly off the clutch, and off we go. Oh, and once you're moving, don't hit anything. Got all that?"

Frank was very surprised when Kate recited the entire procedure back to him without the hesitation. Years ago, when he had received the same short driving lesson on the farm where he had worked during summer break, he'd felt deep trepidation when the old farmer said, "Got all that?" Now he was the old farmer, hoping to have the same impact on Kate, to get her paying attention. Instead, she was ahead of him.

"Wow, Kate, that was perfect. Good girl!"

Frank ran through the procedure a second time, accompanying each step with an action. Finally, the moment came for Frank to push the starter button. Kate squeezed the back of the seat as the machine came to life, feeling the vibration through her feet, and the smell of engine exhaust. Her uncle continued in a louder voice, pointing out oil pressure and coolant temperature instruments. He then moved the throttle a bit, shouting, "Hold on!" when he raised his foot off the clutch and released the brake, causing the tractor to lurch before moving forward just a little faster than a brisk walk.

Kate swiftly understood why she had to hold on tight with her knees slightly bent. However, her biggest concern was the rear wheels turning on each side of her. The fact that the top of each wheel was covered by a small fender did little to reassure her that she wasn't going to be eaten by those giant tires. Thankfully it only took her a minute to realize that there was nothing to this hanging-on thing, and boy, her dad would faint if he saw this!

"How are we doing back there?" Frank yelled over his shoulder.

"Good to go," Kate bellowed back.

"Kate, we have to drive through that muddy area up ahead so I'll have to give it a bit more throttle. Remember to hold tight, and bend your knees a little. Yell if you get scared!"

The tractor continued down the dirt road, flanked by trees leaning in from both sides of the road creating a sort of tunnel. Up ahead, Kate saw the area of mud standing in their way and the water-filled ruts where the tractor had passed on its way to and from the lower vineyard. She realized it might be bumpy and squeezed the back of the seat and bent her knees more than they already were as the tractor began to bog down, its tires sinking into the thick, rich mud. Frank gently pushed the throttle forward, forcing more power from the engine to the rear wheels, which in response bit in with their treads, pushing the tractor forward. Kate heard and felt the power as the tractor shook, sliding to the side, drops of mud and dirty water splattering her as the green machine forged its way forward. Kate smiled, her bent knees and death grip resulting in her not only staying put but enjoying the ride as if at an amusement park.

Climbing out of the mud, Frank backed off the throttle to keep the speed in check, and the two continued their journey through a hayfield into a beautiful vineyard that overlooked another hayfield. Frank pulled the throttle back to idle and pushed down on the clutch and brake at the same time, then flipped the ignition switch in one fluid motion. "Okay, Kate, hop off and we'll get started."

"Wow, that was fun!" Kate exclaimed, not even trying to hide her grin.

"It sure is different from riding in the back seat of a car, isn't it?" her uncle added with a smile.

Time passed quickly while Kate helped her uncle pull black plastic tubing from a reel along the new trestles. After a few rows were pulled, Frank gave Kate the job of fastening the tubing to the lowest of three support wires using plastic clips, while he followed behind punching small holes in the tubing and installing irrigation drippers.

Reaching the end of one row, Kate had the chance to take in the beauty and serenity of the countryside. She loved the quiet rustling of leaves as branches swayed in the soft wind. Everything was so beautiful.

"Uncle Frank, how do you stop animals from eating the grapes?"

Frank stood, wiped his brow, and stretched his back as he looked around. "To tell you the truth, Kate, it's never really been a problem."

"So...no scarecrows?" Kate quipped, remembering how hard she and Jess had laughed.

Frank smiled. "Well, it's time to head back to the house and get cleaned up for dinner, kiddo. How about you take a crack at driving the tractor?"

"What! I can't drive a tractor! I'm...too young," Kate protested, unable to conceal her smile.

Frank laughed. "Nonsense. You climb up on the seat and I'll stand on the bar and talk you through it."

Susan had just finished breading several chicken breasts and putting them into the oven when she heard the familiar sound of the tractor coming up the road. Stepping out onto the porch, she was not surprised to see Kate at the wheel, wearing the biggest grin Sue had seen all day. The tractor stopped in front of the house and idled as Frank talked Kate through the shutdown procedure.

"I must say, I'm impressed!" Sue shouted, putting her hands on her hips.

Frank gave Kate a hand getting down from the now quiet machine, followed by a slapping high five. "I told you; you could do it."

Kate rushed up the porch steps and gave her aunt a big hug. "I can't believe I just drove for the first time—and I drove through the mud, Aunt Sue!"

"I kind of figured something was up when your uncle insisted, I buy you those boots," Sue remarked, exchanging a knowing look with her smiling husband.

"You can't expect me to do all the work around here," Frank retorted.

"Come on in and get cleaned up for dinner, you two. I have chicken baking in the oven."

"I can't wait to tell my mom!" Kate headed into the house.

"How about we keep the tractor thing between us until your parents come up for a visit? I want to see the look on your dad's face when he sees you climb up on that thing and drive away," Frank suggested.

40

"Yes!" Kate yelped. "That's a great idea, Uncle Frank. I won't say a word to either of them!"

Everyone laughed and agreed to keep the secret for the big day. "Okay, tractor girl," Sue ordered with a smile, "go and get cleaned up for dinner. And take those dirty boots off—your uncle isn't the only one who needs some help around here."

Every day for the next week, Kate drove the tractor, with her uncle standing right behind her. Frank explained how to keep safe while adding fuel, and how to connect and engage the mower. She even learned how to cut an open field by starting along the left side, then down the middle, shifting to the right after each pass, making each turn radius the same. At the end of the week, Frank drove Kate out to the tractor, which was already sitting in the largest of the fields. He stayed in the pickup as his niece walked around to his open window, and said, "Kate, I need to run into town, why don't you take care of this field for me. Just don't hit anything," then drove away.

Kate stood rooted—for the first time, she was alone, just her and the tractor. For a moment she thought she would lose her nerve. This was an expensive machine! But her uncle's confidence was contagious and she didn't want to let him down. So she climbed up and positioned herself behind the wheel, then, taking a deep breath, pushed her right foot down on the brake, pushed her left foot down on the clutch, and turned the key. But before pushing the starter button, she paused...just to savor the moment, a moment she wanted to remember.

Chapter 4:
Blue Sky

Kate had just completed mowing the field and was seated on the now quiet machine drinking from her water bottle when she heard the faint sound of an airplane somewhere overhead. It took a moment of searching to find the small yellow craft, high above. Kate smiled at the sight, then her mouth fell open when suddenly the plane's left wing dropped, followed by the nose, as the aircraft entered a spin. Kate couldn't believe her eyes! Then, just moments after completing several complete turns, the little yellow plane stopped spinning and pulled out of its dive. She heard its engine come back to life and relaxed in relief that, for the moment at least, the poor pilot high above her would be spared.

But just as she finished the thought, the plane fell off on the other wing and started spinning in the opposite direction. This time, however, recovery from the spin was followed by a loop. Kate stared skyward in amazement as the small plane returned to straight and level flight and continued on its way. She sat there, not believing what she'd just witnessed, until the sound of her uncle's pickup brought her back to the moment.

"Uncle Frank, I just saw an airplane spin!" she yelled, hopping off the tractor. "It was amazing, and just like that it flew away!"

"Was it in trouble?"

"No, it straightened out and just flew away. I think he did it on purpose," Kate answered, still looking skyward.

"Well, there's an airport not too far from here. We pass it when we drive north to the gas station," Frank offered, looking up, trying to catch a glimpse of the plane.

"Do you think that's where it came from?" Kate asked in a way that told Frank she was interested.

"I'll tell you what. Tomorrow we'll take a ride over there and see if we can find out where the plane came from. Right now, however, we need to get up to the house and clean up because after dinner we're going to the ice cream parlor for sundaes."

"That sounds like fun, what's the occasion?" Kate asked, climbing into the truck. "No occasion, kiddo, we just want to enjoy the sunset from the back deck of the ice cream shop, and thank you for being such a big help this week. Oh, by the way—great job cutting the grass!"

Later that evening, Sue led Kate out onto the deck behind the ice cream parlor, sundaes in hand, and grabbed a seat next to the railing overlooking the rear of the property. The back deck offered a nice view to the southwest and was always a great spot to watch the sunset, and the timing could not have been more perfect, as the high clouds were already turning pink. Off to the west, a thin layer of clouds ran to the horizon, promising to turn the sun's final rays bright red as it sank out of sight. Sue sat quietly waiting for Kate to finish texting.

"Kate, you're going to miss the sunset."

"I'm sorry, Aunt Sue, I just needed to finish that last

one." Kate put her phone down and started anew on her sundae, admiring the high, wispy clouds.

"There," she yelled, pointing. "There's the plane I told you about!"

Less than a mile away, a small yellow plane only a few hundred feet in the air was headed right toward them, descending as it came. Kate was able to see the flaps move as the plane made a left turn and disappeared behind a hill.

"What's all the commotion back here, girls?" Frank inquired, sundae in hand.

"Kate just saw the plane again," Sue replied as Frank took a seat next to her.

"It flew right over our heads and went over those trees," Kate added, pointing with her spoon. "And it was very low."

"It's probably landing at the airport I told you about," Frank speculated as he dug into his dessert. "It's only two miles from here in that direction." He pointed north. "Can you imagine how nice it must be to fly on such a beautiful evening? Look at the mountains, Kate, you're going to miss the sunset."

And the sunset did not disappoint, turning the sky a blazing red, as high clouds accented the scene with bright pinks and purples.

In her nightly call home, Kate confessed, "Mom, I've had such a fun week."

"I know, dear; I've been talking to your aunt every day. She told me you're helping out and having fun. Honey, we're both elated that you're enjoying your time in

Napa. Now off to sleep with you. I love you."

"I love you too, Mom. Good night."

Anna hung up the phone and paused. The guilt she had been dealing with, while not gone, was starting to give way to relief. She walked over to her husband and kissed him on the cheek.

The following morning dawned as beautiful as the last, sunbeams streaming through Kate's blinds and shining right onto her sleeping face. Kate turned over in an attempt to shield her eyes, hoping for a few more minutes of sleep, then remembered her uncle's promise to take her to the airport. Kate sprang out of bed, walked over, and raised the blinds, revealing what she already knew. Another beautiful day.

"Well, here's our farmhand now," Sue announced as Kate came down the stairs.

"Good morning, honey," Frank added, lowering the morning paper and giving Kate a big smile. Kate fixed herself a bowl of cereal and joined her aunt and uncle at the table. "Kate, why don't you stay around the house this morning and give your aunt a hand. I have to go to the motor vehicle office to renew my driver's license. Then after lunch you can take a ride with me. I have to see Ned Baker, who runs Vineland's Best vineyard. His place is just north of that airport I told you about. I can drop you off at the airport and pick you up on the way back."

"What should I do there? I don't know anyone."

Frank thought about it for a moment. "I know there's an office, and I always see cars in the parking lot. Just go in and ask about the plane you saw. I'm sure everyone will be very nice, and you might make a few new friends. I'll call you on your cell on my way back to the airport. How does that sound?"

"How long be before you pick me up?" Kate asked, trying to get her head around what to expect.

"About an hour," Frank replied. "That should give you some time to look around. What do you think?"

"Sounds okay to me, just don't forget me there," Kate said, smiling with a mouth full of cereal.

Chapter 5:
Questions

Kate was a little apprehensive as her uncle drove away, leaving her in front of the Clearview Airport office. Kate loved being treated like a grown-up, and her uncle's confidence seemed to be rubbing off. She walked toward the office, looking forward to having an intelligent conversation with someone, she just didn't know who.

Kate opened the screen door and walked in and looked around. The walls were covered with pictures of aircraft past and present. As Kate studied the pictures, it became clear that the airport's better days were already behind it. Some pictures showed cars from long ago parked alongside hangars with men and women dressed much differently from today. The main hangar looked freshly painted and was surrounded by planes of all shapes and sizes waiting their chance to grace the sky.

Now, dusty model airplanes hung from the office ceiling, a coffeemaker sat on a small table against the far wall, the nondairy creamer and a few dirty spoons there to keep it company. In the center of the office stood a wooden table, the many scratches attesting to its long life, with a lone coffee cup filled with pens and pencils serving as the centerpiece. But to Kate's amazement, there was no one in the office. Sure, there on the counter a pen and pad sat at the ready and on the desk behind the counter sat a laptop, and the plant on the windowsill was healthy, but no one was around.

"Hello?" Kate called out, then listened. "Hello, anyone home?"—this time louder. Kate studied the office for a few more minutes, waiting for someone to show up before deciding to go out the back screen door and look around for someone outside. She found herself looking out at the airport grounds. In front of her was a large paved area, a gas pump off to the right, and a white and orange plane parked off to the far left. Further to the left, lined up like dominoes, she saw long green one-story buildings with large white doors. Kate had seen them from the main road before turning into the airport parking lot, her uncle identifying them as hangars. The runway, which ran from left to right, had a grassy area separating the paved area with the gas pump from the runway. Off to the right stood the main hangar depicted in the pictures in the office, rust now covering the walls where paint had flaked off.

Kate remembered seeing a door open on one of the hangars as her uncle drove up. *Someone has to be here somewhere*, she thought, and with an hour to kill Kate decided to investigate. She walked along a narrow road that ran behind the end of the hangars until coming to the hangar with the open door at the far end. Again Kate announced her presence with a loud hello, yet still there was no response. As Kate walked between the hangars toward the open door, the nose of an airplane with a wooden propeller became visible. Each step allowed more of the airplane to come into view, until Kate could see that the plane was indeed yellow, and might be the plane she

48

had seen the other day.

She walked up to the open hangar and just stood there, staring. The yellow plane before her was larger than she'd imagined and seemed to have its nose pointed toward the sky, its tail sitting low to the ground, unlike the plane sitting by the office.

"Hello?" she called out again, stepping closer to the front of the aircraft. Kate inspected the propeller, admiring its polished wood, which resembled a fine piece of furniture, its many layers forming graceful lines along its length. The tip and front edge of each blade were covered with shiny metal, molded to fit perfectly, the edges blending seamlessly where metal and wood met. As Kate ran her hand along the polished wood she noticed her reflection in the shiny chrome spinner covering the propeller hub. She peered at her reflection in the mirrorlike finish, which reminded her of Christmas tree ornaments. She moved her face closer, amused at how large and distorted her nose looked, then moved back, watching her reflection change.

Startled by movement behind her, Kate spun to her right to find a man, several feet away between the two hangars, arms crossed, watching her! He was an older man, tall with a full head of gray hair and blue eyes. His old jeans, tan collared shirt with pockets on both sides, and work boots convinced Kate that he was here a lot.

"You can look all you want, but you shouldn't touch unless you have permission," the man said in a pleasant tone.

"I'm sorry; I was just looking for someone to talk to

about airplanes, but no one was around. Is this your plane?" Kate asked as she composed herself.

"Michelle the airport manager had to run Bob the mechanic over to the post office, that's why the office is empty, plus it's a weekday, that's why it's so quiet around here, and yes, this is my plane." He wiped his hands with a rag as he walked past Kate toward an old table and chair located against the wall. "Are you here with someone, missy?"

Kate followed the man toward the side of the hangar but remained outside. "My name is Kate; I'm staying with my aunt and uncle this summer. I think I saw you fly over their vineyard yesterday, and again last evening. Oh, and I'm fifteen."

"Well, all grown-up, are you," the man said with a chuckle. "Yep, that was me. I changed the oil and put in a new set of spark plugs yesterday then went up to check out how old Annabelle here ran. My name's Jake." The tall gentleman put his rag on the table and walked over to Kate and shook her hand. "So where are your folks?"

"I live in LA with my mom and dad, but I'm spending the summer with my uncle Frank and aunt Susan. He owns Hilltop Vineyards. He just drove over to Vineland's Best vineyard and dropped me off for an hour so I could take a look around and talk to people about flying."

Kate stopped for a moment as she realized that it was the thought of flying and not just airplanes that drew her to this place.

"So you want to fly?" Jake asked, walking over to

50

the left wing. "Well, missy, help me pull this old bird out of the nest and I'll show you a few things about airplanes. Just pull right here." Jake patted his hand on the left strut that held the wing up. "I'll go over to the other side and we can pull together."

"How hard is it to move?" Kate asked as Jake reached the other side and grabbed the right strut.

"Just pull so we keep the plane going straight, it's not that heavy. Ready? Pull!"

Kate was surprised when she saw her wing moving backward. *Pull hard!* she thought as she put her back into it. The plane began moving forward toward the opening and into the sunlight. Kate found that after the initial effort to get things started, the plane did indeed roll easily.

"That's far enough, now start pushing back and we'll swing her around."

Kate pushed hard as Jake continued to pull, causing the plane to pirouette to the left.

"That's fine, Kate, thank you. Now come over to this side and I'll explain a few things to you."

As she hurried around the front of the small yellow plane, Kate could not believe her luck. This was the plane she had seen, and now she was talking to the pilot!

"Let's start over here by the cockpit," Jake said as he lifted the window on the side of the fuselage and lowered the half door.

Kate hurried around and stood behind the right wing close to the narrow cockpit before Jake continued.

"As you can see this plane has two seats, one behind the other, and separate flight controls for each occupant. The front and rear sticks are connected to each other and control the aileron on the back of each wing."

Jake moved the front stick left and right, causing the rear stick and the large panels on each wing to move.

"Kate, notice how the ailerons move in opposite directions. As we fly, the down aileron increases lift on that wing, while the up aileron decreases lift on the other wing. That's how we bank the aircraft to make a turn."

"Now watch the tail for a moment." He moved the stick fore and aft. "That back there is the elevator," he explained as the horizontal surface at the tail of the plane pivoted up and down. "It's used to control the pitch of the nose up and down as we fly, which in turn changes the angle of the wing in relation to the air that it's flying through. And last but not least, these pedals on the floor are used to move the rudder; it's used to yaw the airplane side to side." Jake moved one of the foot pedals with his hand, causing the rudder to swing left and right.

"Why would you want to fly the airplane sideways?" Kate asked, fully invested in understanding what the flight controls did.

"When we start a right turn, for instance, the down aileron, lifting the left wing, catches more air and gets pushed backward, causing the nose of the airplane to swing, or yaw, to the left. We call that adverse yaw. We use the rudder to overcome the adverse yaw and keep the plane pointing in the direction of the turn."

After a long moment, Kate looked at Jake. "So, to make a right turn, the right wing goes down and the left wing goes up, but the left wing gets pulled back, which we prevent with the rudder. Yeah, I got it."

Jake straightened up and looked at her in disbelief. "You got it right, just like that? Wow, smart kid."

He finished up their walk-around by explaining the air speed indicator and altimeter on the instrument panel before walking around to the front of the yellow plane. "What do you think, Kate?"

Kate was ecstatic. "Thank you so much, Mr. Jake!"

"I'll tell you what, missy. If you can talk your parents into giving their permission, you can accompany me on an evening flight sometime next week."

Kate's smile lit up her face. "Really? Wow—how cool is that!" Kate pumped her fist as if she had just struck out a batter. "I'll ask my mother and let you know right away." She started running toward the office. It took a few steps for Kate's brain to catch up with her feet...she skidded to a stop.

"Wait," she said, spinning back to Jake. "I won't talk to my mom until tonight, is that okay?"

Jake just stood in amazement, having not expected such an animated reaction to his suggestion. "Sure, it's okay, missy, but calm down a minute and come back over here. It would help if I give you my phone number."

Kate walked back, feeling foolish for the moment, but still wearing a smile. "I guess that would help. I'm sorry."

"Heck, there's no need to apologize about being excited. I didn't sleep a wink the night before I got to take my first airplane ride." Jake reached into his wallet and handed Kate a business card.

"I've been in a jet, so I know what it's like to fly," Kate volunteered, trying to sound worldly.

"That's good," Jake encouraged, "but this will be a bit different. Did they let you fly the jet?"

"You're going to let me fly?" Kate gasped. "Is that allowed?"

"Sure, it's allowed, missy, so ask your parents, and let them know they should feel free to give me a call."

"Thank you, Mr. Jake!" Kate replied as she spun again for the office.

Chapter 6:
Water Under the Bridge

Jake smiled as he watched the teenager walk toward the office, but only for a moment before pushing the plane back into the hangar. He walked to the side of the hangar and picked up the rag off his desk; but it was too late, his smile began to fade. Jake stared off into space as painful memories, kept at bay for years, came flooding back. It was as if the girl had opened the door to that dreadful vault where Jake had locked the memories away for so long.

Jake had learned to fly back in the 1960s from a dirt strip in Fresno at the age of sixteen. He got a job after school to pay for a one-hour lesson once a week in a plane just like the one sitting in front of him. After graduation, Jake started flying UH-1 "Huey" helicopters after enlisting in the Army's warrant officer flight training program and was shipped off to Vietnam. He was assigned to the 101st Cavalry, flying troops into and out of forward areas. Many more times than he wanted to remember, Jake had flown his Huey into hot landing zones to evacuate wounded comrades. The mission that still haunted him had begun when Jake, his copilot Phil Dysart, and door gunner John Bell were headed toward an area in the Central Highlands with three other choppers to deliver ammunition and evacuate the wounded, even though a fierce battle was still raging. Phil Dysart was a very funny guy from

Mississippi, and John Bell, who grew up hunting in the backwoods of Ohio, could shoot a deer two hundred yards away.

It was easy to locate the area where the battle was; plumes of smoke billowing through the thick canopy of trees could be seen ten miles away. Radio chatter from troops on the ground painted a picture of a vicious battle with the enemy. As Jake began descending, he made note of possible forced-landing sites. He could see Zebra One Five, an American artillery base off to his left, not three miles from his location, its artillery firing toward the distant hilltops. Things began to happen fast as Jake, who was to be the first chopper in, made his approach into a small clearing where troops had set off a green smoke grenade to mark the landing zone. "This is gonna be hot, Phil—see there off to the south, enemy mortar shells hitting our boys." Jake then called back on the intercom to his door gunner. He often alerted John to approaching targets so John could be ready to take them under fire with his M60 machine gun as they flew by. "John, clearing coming up—gooks in the open in three, two, one!"

John opened up even before he spotted the clearing, his murderous fire ripping into the exposed enemy as he swung the machine gun around.

"Okay, boys, here we go," Jake warned as he brought his chopper in so hot that he almost stood it on its tail to stop its forward motion, causing a huge cloud of debris to fill the cabin. The Huey landed hard, and John started kicking crates of ammunition out the left side of the cabin as soldiers loaded four wounded men in from

56

the right. A moment later, bullets began hitting the Huey. "They're right in that tree line!" Phil yelled, pointing over his right shoulder.

To Jake, every second on the ground felt like an eternity, until John yelled for him to get out of there. Jake added all the power the engine could deliver and raised the collective, changing the pitch of the rapidly spinning blades. He lifted the helicopter off the ground and spun around in one graceful motion, the tail rising as he pushed the stick forward to gain speed. But before the chopper could gain altitude, bullets shattered the windshield, one ripping through Phil's chest as additional rounds poured into the cockpit.

Jake fought for control of the wounded bird. Every red light on the instrument panel warned of impending engine failure. Jake pushed the transmit button and shouted to the other choppers, "They're behind you, enemy to your rear!"

He looked over at Phil slumped in his seat, blood soaking his uniform. Smoke filled the cabin while violent vibrations began shaking the stricken bird apart. Hoping to put some distance between himself and the enemy, and knowing that the end was near, Jake stayed as close to the treetops as possible to make the coming crash survivable. Smoke was everywhere, the acrid particles filling Jake's lungs, the vibrations so bad Jake knew the aircraft was coming apart in the air. He called back to his door gunner. Getting no response, Jake looked behind him. John was no longer in the aircraft. Then as Jake added pressure on the right foot pedal, the shaft connecting the tail rotor to the engine failed, causing the craft to spin around uncontrollably as it crashed through the treetops, coming to rest on its side.

Heat...darkness...

Heat was the first sensation Jake felt. He was on his side, pain shooting through his right leg. It took a moment for Jake to come to his senses. The realization that the enemy would be on him in moments pumped adrenaline through his body like a fire hose. There was no more pain, no confusion, just action. Jake ripped off his helmet and straps and looked for his copilot, finding an empty space where the seat had been. He climbed out of the wreckage and looked to see if anyone else had survived. One of the wounded was lying in mud less than twenty feet from where he stood. Wasting no time, Jake picked up the unconscious man and carried him a safe distance from the chopper. Jake dropped the man to the ground and had turned to go back for the others when the helicopter exploded, knocking him off his feet, as burning fuel sent a huge fireball up through the thick jungle canopy.

Knowing that the enemy would soon converge on their location, Jake turned to grab the wounded man just as shots rang out. Jake felt pain erupt in his left arm and heard the snap of bullets passing his head as he pulled the wounded man onto his back. Then disappeared into the jungle, carrying the wounded soldier as fast as possible toward the firebase he had flown past on his way in. It took two hours before the exhausted pilot reached the perimeter of the base, and another twenty minutes to drag the wounded man close enough to yell for help without being shot by jumpy sentries guarding its perimeter.

Finally close enough to hear voices, Jake yelled for help.

The voices stopped, then after a long moment came, "Who's Mickey Mantle?"

"Mickey Mantle—Mickey Mantle!—get over here and help me with this wounded man, you idiot!"

"Okay, okay, you're American!"

"Damn right I am!"

As Jake was being carried to the first aid area, the sentry asked how he was doing.

"Well, I'm still alive and kicking—mostly kicking."

The soldier he'd carried for hours did survive; and, after recovering from his own wounds, Jake finished his tour of duty. However, Jake's copilot Phil and door gunner John had been killed in action.

When his tour in Vietnam ended, Jake came back to the States to pursue a career as a commercial helicopter pilot. Along the way, he earned his commercial fixed-wing license to fly airplanes and, after three years as a part-time flight instructor, he was hired by the airlines. About that time, he met his soon-to-be wife, Marie, working as a flight attendant for the same airline. Marie, a petite blonde, liked Jake the first time they met and agreed to marry him after dating for three months. Their daughter, Mary, was born a year later; however, the fairy-tale life that was unfolding in front of the couple came crashing down around them when it was discovered that Mary had been born with a severe heart defect.

To Jake, his daughter Mary was the most beautiful baby he had ever seen. He spent every moment he had playing with her, making her laugh, and giving her his best, all the while knowing that her life might be cut short. Jake and Marie did everything they could for their daughter, providing a loving environment and the best medical care, while exhausting their energy looking for a way to stop their daughter's affliction from sapping life from her. In the end, Mary lost her battle at the age of seven, which in turn left Marie and Jake emotionally unable to cope with her loss.

After a year's leave of absence from the airline, Jake returned to the job he loved, but the pain he carried around with him had changed him into a different person. Once fun-loving and outgoing, Jake was distant, and always angry. Marie hung on for five years trying to make their marriage work before filing for divorce. After that, Jake spent the remainder of his airline career living alone and purchased the yellow Piper Cub as a retirement gift to himself.

The sound of an airplane taking off brought Jake back to the present. He looked down and reflected on the young girl he had just met. The kid's enthusiasm made him smile.

Frank couldn't stop smiling as he made the turn into the vineyard. Kate hadn't come up for air the whole ride home, explaining how ailerons and elevators did this and that, how heavy the plane was, and how lucky she was to meet the pilot. Frank stopped the truck in front of the house and looked at Kate. "Go tell Aunt Sue about your adventure and give your mom a call when she gets home, so we can get things started." Frank watched as Kate ran into the house. "This might be a good thing," he said to himself before joining the women inside.

For the remainder of the week, Kate could not stop looking at the sky. She smiled, remembering her mother's reaction, and how jealous her father was, after hearing that the pilot was going to let her fly the plane. Uncle Frank had assured Anna that everything was going to be fine, but it still took a while before her mother reluctantly agreed, with both parents leaving it up to Frank to make the arrangements.

That weekend, Sue made plans to introduce Kate to the family across the road in hopes of connecting her with a few high school students in the area. The Gillmans owned Rosewood Vineyards and were active at the high school their son Bruce attended.

Arriving at the Gillmans' with her aunt, Kate admired the simple beauty of their home and the wonderful panorama of vineyard-covered hills. It took a moment for Laura, a tall and slender blond-haired woman, to answer the door.

"Hello there, you must be Kate. Please come in. Hi, Sue, how's Frank?"

"He's doing great, Laura. How is Roger doing with his back? Frank told me he pulled it unloading the pickup the other day."

"He did, but luckily he's fine. Come into the kitchen, I'd like to introduce you to my son, Bruce."

Kate was happy to just stay at her aunt and uncle's

for the summer and couldn't shake the feeling that she was an imposition. Too bad the Gillmans didn't have a daughter. Kate followed behind her aunt into the kitchen, getting a peek as they entered. Bruce, who was seated at the table, stood and shook Kate's and Sue's hands, but didn't utter a sound.

"Bruce," said Laura, "Kate is spending the summer with Frank and Susan. I think it would be nice if the two of you attend the fair together this coming weekend. I know you were planning to meet some friends there. You can introduce Kate."

Kate and Bruce looked at each other, both feeling awkward at the arranged meeting. Laura put out some cake and milk for Kate and Bruce and invited Susan out onto the deck where she had some lemonade waiting. Kate and Bruce sat quietly at first, eating cake and drinking milk, until Bruce took a slug of milk that went down the wrong way, causing him to choke and cough at the same time. Milk gushed out of his nose and into the napkin he had grabbed.

Kate was shocked and didn't know whether to laugh or run, and poor Bruce, humiliated for the moment, finally opened his eyes. The two looked at each other and broke out into laughter. After that, there was no holding back as stories of epic fails flew back and forth. Hearing the laughter, Laura and Sue looked at each other and smiled.

After an hour, Sue and Kate said their good-byes, and Kate immediately called her mother and relived the entire episode over the phone as they drove home, then spent the evening texting with her friends about how comfortable she felt with Bruce, and about the prospect of spending the day with him at a fair and meeting other kids.

The next morning, Kate was greeted by low clouds clinging to the treetops as she drove the tractor into the lower vineyard, then stopped to watch as the gentle breeze sent puffs of cloud up into the air like cotton candy. While viewing the beautiful countryside, Kate pondered the events of the last few days, feeling a sense of anticipation and excitement as she thought about her upcoming trip to the airport and the fair.

Chapter 7:
A Day at the Fair

Frank's pickup made a right into the Napa Valley fairgrounds. The truck containing a very nervous Kate Wilson, and driven by an equally nervous Sue Wilson came to a stop under the shade of one of the only trees in the parking lot.

"Remember, Kate, this is no big deal. Bruce's mom told me before they left that Bruce is very well-mannered, and is as nervous as you are. When they get here, the four of us will walk around together for a while. Laura and I intend to go off together after a few minutes, so you kids can go off and have fun. Unfortunately, the friends Bruce was planning to meet had other plans, so it will probably just be you and him."

Kate felt her stomach tighten; things had changed into an almost date. "There's plenty to do," her aunt continued, "even though the fairgrounds aren't that big. We'll meet back at the gate at 7:00 p.m. sharp. Okay?"

"Okay, Aunt Sue, but do I pay for things that I want to do, or does Bruce?"

"Well, you shouldn't expect Bruce to pay, but if he offers, by all means let him. But it wouldn't hurt if you paid for him some of the time. The best thing to do is just be yourself, be a good listener, and have fun. Don't try to be someone you're not. I tried that once."

"So what happened?"

64

"After a few minutes, I forgot who I was trying to be! Very embarrassing." Both women laughed.

Laura and Bruce pulled up a few minutes later, and Sue gave Kate a nudge as they watched Bruce's mom give him last-minute instructions before they got out of the car. The four met at the ticket counter, where Laura insisted on buying tickets for everyone, and it wasn't long before Laura and Sue decided to go into the vendors' pavilion to look at handmade quilts and bags.

"So, Kate, this whole thing feels awkward," Bruce finally said as they walked.

Kate smiled. "Yeah, a little, but don't let that throw you. I'll bet I can still beat you at that ball-throwing thing over there."

Kate held her breath, not believing her boldness. But Bruce had a big smile on his face.

"Okay, Kate, deal it up," Bruce challenged at the first game booth. Kate looked at the ball, aimed, and threw as hard as she could. The ball went straight up, hitting the ceiling and almost hit the man running the game. Kate covered her mouth as Bruce and the man laughed.

"See? I told you I was good, bet you can't beat that," Kate responded with a bit of moxie, happy at how easy it was to make Bruce laugh. Bruce didn't hit anything, either, and both agreed it was better to just get some cotton candy, walk around, and go on a few rides.

"So how do you like staying at the vineyard all summer?" Bruce asked.

Kate thought about it a moment. "I didn't like the

idea at first, but my aunt and uncle are great people and I'm doing things I've never even dreamed of, and now I might fly a plane. Plus they treat me like a grown-up. But I do miss my mom and dad."

Bruce smiled. "Flying a plane sounds awesome, just don't throw up."

Kate laughed and promised she wouldn't.

Bruce then said, "I'll bet the longest I was away from my parents was a week with the high school softball team, when we made the state playoffs."

Kate teased, "I hope you weren't pitching!"

Bruce just shook his head.

As they walked, the two talked at length about what it was like to grow up where they lived and their thoughts about the future, and what they wanted to do after graduating.

"I'm planning to stay right here in Napa," Bruce said. "I love living here and I love working in the vineyard. People have no idea what it takes to grow quality grapes. Every decision affects the taste of the wine they produce."

"I know what you mean. Uncle Frank has been explaining things to me. It's so complicated."

"What are you thinking about doing?"

"Well, I like the idea of traveling, maybe on a cruise ship, or as an airline flight attendant."

"I like it," Bruce agreed as the pair stopped in front of another ride.

#

At 7:00 on the dot, the two friends showed up at the main gate just as Sue and Laura arrived. "What on earth is hanging from your pants, Bruce?" his mom laughingly yelled as she pointed out the napkin stuck to Bruce's butt. Bruce spun around to look, only to have his butt follow him around in a circle like a dog chasing its tail. This got everyone laughing including Bruce. But Kate lost it when she revealed that she hadn't said a word as payback for Bruce not telling her about her white nose after she finished a waffle cake. Now the four laughed even harder, the laughter continuing until they got back to their cars.

Kate talked and talked as her aunt drove. "You were right, Aunt Sue, Bruce is a nice guy, and I was myself. We agreed that we would buy our own food and Bruce would pay for the rides. Things went a lot better than I thought they would."

"That's wonderful, Kate. Did you talk about your upcoming airplane ride?"

"Yep, he was thrilled, but told me I'd better not throw up in the plane."

"You're not going to get sick, Kate. Did the rides make you sick?"

"I never get sick," Kate replied, "and I love rides, spinning around, going up and down. Wait—Jake isn't going to do any of that stuff, is he?" Kate asked as the reality of her upcoming flight started to sink in.

"Well, before the flight, why don't you talk about anything that concerns you, so you'll know what to expect."

Sue turned off the St. Helena Highway and onto their road. "I know your uncle will be making arrangements with the pilot tomorrow, so you might be going up sometime this week," Sue added before halting the pickup in front of the house.

Frank, hearing the truck, came onto the porch to greet them, eager to hear about the day. That night, Kate texted Jess, then relived every moment with her mom, who was eager to hear the details of her daughter's first date.

"All right, dear, it's getting late, you better get to sleep now and we'll talk about it again tomorrow. Kate, Dad and I miss you and love you so much."

"I love you, too, Mom. Talk to you tomorrow."

After the call, Kate felt like her mom was a lot calmer, and drifted off to sleep that evening to the sound of carnival music playing in her head as she replayed the day over and over. She liked Bruce, and she had gone on her first date, kind of.

The next day, Kate was up with the sun, and as always was greeted with a big smile from her aunt. "Eggs and bacon today for breakfast?" Sue asked as she prepared a plate. "I don't know what your uncle has in store for you today, but he did take special interest in the weather forecast this morning, and was happy when he learned it's going to be a beautiful evening."

Kate's eyes lit up. "I hope today's the day! I'll bet I can get it out of him. Uncle Frank can't keep a secret."

"Well, let's see if you can squeeze it out of him," Sue conspired as she joined Kate at the table.

"Good morning, girls, how did everyone sleep?" Frank greeted as he made his usual entrance through the front door.

"Great, Uncle Frank. Good morning," Kate replied, getting up from her chair to give her uncle a kiss.

"It sure is a beautiful morning, but I thought I heard it's going to rain this evening," Kate observed casually.

"Nonsense. Where did you hear a thing like that? Well, it better not rain," he continued, "because you have an appointment with an airplane this evening, and rain would spoil everything."

Kate's threw her hands in the air as she grinned. "Really! This evening? Does my dad know?"

"Yep, I spoke to him yesterday. He's very excited for you. Jake is going to meet us at the hangar at 6:30 this evening."

Kate gave her uncle a bear hug. "Thank you, Uncle Frank. Wow—I can't wait!"

"Well, I have to drive out to the farm supply store for some hardware before servicing the spray equipment. You can give your aunt a hand, and after lunch you can cut the lower field again."

"Aye, aye, captain," Kate said, standing and saluting as a soldier would.

"At ease, kiddo," Frank said with a smile as he walked across the kitchen to give Sue a peck on the lips before heading out to the truck.

"You're right about your uncle not being able to keep a secret," Sue said, chuckling, as she joined Kate at the table. "Don't worry about helping out in the kitchen. What you can do is call your mother and spend some time with her on the phone. I'm getting the feeling that she's missing you. I know you check in every evening, but a nice long conversation might be just what the doctor ordered for her."

Kate reflected for a moment. "I'm missing her a lot, too. Thanks, a long conversation sounds perfect."

Kate finished her breakfast and headed out to the porch to call her mom.

After lunch, Kate took the tractor and cut the field, pausing occasionally to scan the sky for airplanes. At one point, she wondered if this field was long enough to land a plane on. *What would it be like to land a plane in a field?* she thought as she got back to work in earnest. Kate was so preoccupied thinking about her upcoming flight that she lost track of time.

Sue heard the tractor slowly making its way up from the lower field as she continued on the phone, "I'm sure you have nothing to worry about, Anna," she assured her nervous sister-in-law. "Frank has every confidence in this pilot, and Kate will be fine. And here she is now," Sue finished as Kate walked in. "It's your mother, Kate. Why don't you pick it up in the family room and talk with her again."

Chapter 8:
First Flight

The day started the same way it always did for Jake Hollerman: up early, out to the gym, clean up, then drive to the diner for breakfast. For Chris the server, however, this morning seemed a little different from most. Jake was sitting at his usual spot in the back of the diner, but there was something unusual about him this morning. Something she couldn't put her finger on.

"What will it be, Jake?" she asked loudly over the noise as she hurried by with an order for the couple sitting at a window.

"The usual," Jake answered, his eyes following Chris as she blew past. *Something's up with him this morning, and I'm gonna find out what it is*, she thought with a twinkle in her eye.

Chris poured coffee into Jake's mug, pausing just a moment too long, before turning toward the kitchen.

"What the heck's gotten into you this morning?" Jake asked, smiling, as Chris disappeared. A few minutes later, Chris reappeared with Jake's scrambled eggs, bacon, and home fries. "Blue, your eyes are blue," Jake observed as if it were the first time he had done so.

"Well, there's a news flash, and it only took a year to notice," Chris scolded.

"Okay, don't get all flustered about it," Jake came back, obviously embarrassed she'd heard him.

Jake liked eating breakfast at the diner. The food was good, and Chris always went out of her way to make sure he was given excellent service. One day it finally dawned on him why he liked the diner so much. Chris was the first woman Jake had admired in a long while. The only problem was getting up the nerve to ask her out, or, for that matter, just carry on a conversation.

Chris saw Jake finishing up and quickly reached into her apron, walked over, and placed his cheek on the table. "So, Jake, you look like the cat that ate the canary. Has a lady caught your eye?"

"Now if I told you that, you girls would try to figure out who it was all day instead of serving the customers," Jake answered, not wanting to give Chris any fuel for speculation.

"That's okay. Lynn, the evening server, told me she knows who it is, but that little witch won't tell me," Chris lamented. "Anyway, have a nice day, Jake, see you tomorrow."

She winked and walked away, proud of how she'd handled herself. The truth was that Chris had realized several months ago that she was a little too happy whenever Jake came in and disappointed when he didn't.

As Jake grabbed his hat and headed for the door, he couldn't help but take one last look at her.

The evening was as beautiful as forecast, with light winds and high wispy clouds. After leaving the diner, Jake had spent the day cleaning the Cub and updating his logbook. His dinner consisted of a half-eaten meatball sub, a bottle of water, and two packs of cheese-filled crackers from the vending machine in the airport lobby, where Michelle, the airport manager, gave Jake a hard time about the upcoming flight.

"I'm sure the kid will appreciate how shiny your plane looks," the tall, thin woman said. "Besides, polishing makes all the difference in how it flies."

Jake laughed at the sarcastic remark. He loved giving Michelle a hard time and could take a good dig every now and then. Like he told her on several occasions, "A good dig once in a while keeps me on my toes. I never hold back about your big feet, so fire away."

Frank Wilson turned his pickup into the airport parking lot, thrilled that his niece had the perfect weather for her adventure. Kate smiled as she caught a glimpse of the yellow plane in front of Jake's open hangar just before the truck entered the parking lot. "There it is!" she shouted, pointing toward the long buildings.

After parking, Frank and Susan followed Kate around the back of the first hangar to where the yellow plane sat waiting.

Jake was standing in front of the Cub wiping a bug he had missed on the chrome spinner when he heard footsteps.

"Wow, Mr. Jake, it looks beautiful!" Jake looked up as Kate, her aunt, and uncle walked around to the front of the plane. "Hello, Jake. Frank Wilson, and this is my wife, Susan." Frank extended his hand.

"Hello, Frank, Susan, pleased to meet you," Jake answered, shaking their hands with a firm grip. "Well, Kate, it's good to see you again. I understand we're going flying."

"Thank you for doing this for me, Mr. Jake," was all Kate could get out.

"Don't thank me until it's over," the big man said dryly.

"Looks like the perfect evening for a flight," Sue observed, looking up at the sky.

"Yep, it's a good one, so let's get started. Kate, why don't you walk around with me as we preflight the airplane, then we'll strap in and go flying."

Kate looked at her aunt and uncle. Both were wearing the biggest grins.

"Kate, this aircraft is a Piper J3 Cub and was built in 1946. Between 1938 and 1947, almost twenty thousand were built in Lock Haven, Pennsylvania. It features a tubular steel frame fuselage covered by fabric, has a four-cylinder engine, and very good handling characteristics. All right, Kate, let's begin by walking around the aircraft to see if it's safe to get into. Frank, you and Sue can follow along, and Frank, I'm giving you the job of pulling the chocks after I start the engine. They're connected to this rope, so stand well off to the side and pull them over to you once I'm in and buckled up."

Kate listened and observed, from tires to tail feathers, with Jake explaining everything he looked at along the way. Finally her big moment came.

"All right, Kate, it's time for you to get in," Jake said. "This airplane was designed to be flown solo from the back seat, so you're sitting up front. Climb up on the front tire, then sit on the edge of the plane and wiggle yourself onto the seat."

Kate stepped up onto the tire holding whatever was within reach. She turned her back to the plane and slid her butt onto the front seat then positioned her legs on each side of the control stick while getting her first closeup view of the vintage flying machine's interior.

It was small. The well-worn black floor was dirty, and exposed cables that connected the front and rear rudder pedals rubbed against Kate's ankles. The sides of the cockpit were covered with the same yellow fabric as the outside, sporting knobs and cranks built into black metal pockets. To her front, two metal bars ran up from the sides of the black instrument panel, which was adorned with several round instruments. It was nothing like she had imagined.

Jake came alongside, instructing her on the proper way to fasten her seat belt and helped her put on a headset, complete with a microphone boom. Jake plugged the headset into the intercom jacks on the left side of the cockpit, then instructed Kate on how to undo her seat belt and get out of the plane in case of emergency.

"Okay, missy, see those small pedals on the floor in front of the rudder pedals? They're heel brakes. Using your heels, push both of them forward, and hold the plane from moving while I start the engine. Okay, are you all set?"

Kate, filled with anticipation, pressed hard against the pedals with both heels. "Okay, sir." She nodded. Jake walked to the front and tried pushing the small plane back, checking that the wheels were indeed locked. He then came alongside the cockpit, reached over to the instrument panel, turned a silver knob labeled "Primer," and pumped the knob in and out a few times.

"This primer squirts fuel into the engine to help get it started," Jake explained as he pushed the knob back and turned it to lock it in place. "Now I'm turning the magnetos on. When I spin the prop, the magnetos will generate high voltage and send it to the spark plugs at just the right moment to start the engine. Before I do that, I want you to look around and make sure no one is near the plane. When you're sure it's safe, I want you to yell the word 'Clear!' nice and loud."

Kate looked around then bellowed, "Clear!"

Jake checked to see that Frank and Sue were out of the way, reached forward with his right hand, grabbed the propeller blade in front of him, and with a swift downward thrust, spun the propeller. The engine coughed to life, shaking the plane before it settled into a soft, slow idle as Jake climbed into the back seat and buckled up. Kate, still diligently holding the brakes, and listening to how smooth the engine ran, was startled when Jake's voice came through her headset asking if she was all set to go. "Yes, I am, sir!"

"Kate, can you hear me, are you ready to go?" Jake asked again. "Move the microphone closer to your mouth and try again. You should hear your voice through the ear cups as you speak."

Kate adjusted the boom so the small sponge sleeve covering the microphone was almost touching her lip. "Yes, Mr. Jake, I'm all set." This time Kate could hear herself.

"Great, missy. You can take your feet off the brakes, I have them, so now let's begin. I'll add a bit of power, release the brakes, and start to taxi forward." Jake gave Frank the signal to pull the chocks from the front of the wheels.

"Kate, I steer the plane by pushing the rudder pedals with my feet. Left rudder to go left, right rudder to go right. The brakes you were using to hold the plane work independently, so you can also use them to help maneuver while taxiing. Remember, the tail is swinging around behind us, so we have to be mindful not to hit anything with it."

"Okay, Mr. Jake, but I can't see what's ahead of us with the nose tilted up in front of me," Kate replied.

"You're right, missy. Let me demonstrate how it's done. First we hold the stick all the way back to our belly. This way the prop blast will hold the tail wheel tight to the ground. Then we move the black knob on your left marked "Throttle" forward a bit to increase power." Jake inched the throttle forward.

As the plane began rolling, Kate gave her aunt and uncle a quick thumbs-up.

"In a taildragger, we make small S-turns, swinging the nose to the left and right, allowing us a glimpse forward for a moment as the nose swings out of the way. Let me demonstrate, then you can try it."

Using the rudder pedals, Jake swung the nose from side to side like a drunken goose, letting Kate see past the nose to the left, then the right as the plane moved along the taxiway at a slow and cautious pace. Jake stopped the plane. "Okay, Kate, heels on the brakes, toes on the rudder pedals, and hold the stick in your belly, I'll control the throttle."

Kate eased off the brakes and felt the plane begin to move, then pushed the left rudder pedal. The plane promptly wandered off the taxiway and onto the grass. Kate was lost; it was almost impossible to apply brakes while steering with the rudder, and now the plane was rocking side to side.

"Stay with it, Kate—get off the brakes and give it a jab of right rudder, but be ready with a jab to the left as soon as we get back onto the hardtop," Jake coached.

Kate leaned over, looking out to the sides as the plane again began to move. "That's it. Right rudder, now straight, now jab left, now straight, now a jab right, now left." The Cub rolled back onto the taxiway and moved in the right direction. Kate found it hard, but she was doing it, shaky at first but more precise with each cycle.

"Okay, missy, let's stop here by using the heel brakes again, and we'll do our run-up."

Kate hadn't expected how physical taxiing the aircraft could be. Those heel brakes, the noise and vibration of the engine, the rocking of the plane as it rolled off the taxiway onto the grass, and of course pushing on the rudder pedals. Her legs really got a workout.

This was nothing like she had imagined. Heck, the tractor was easy compared to this! But she did it.

"Earth to Kate, Earth to Kate, you still with me, missy?"

"It was hard keeping the plane on the taxiway," was all she could respond with.

"You did great for the first time. Heck, by the time we get back to the hangar, you'll be a pro," Jake replied. "Let's begin our run-up and see if this plane is safe to fly. This engine has two separate ignition systems with their own set of spark plugs for each cylinder. We have to prove that both sets are working before we can take off. I'll do that by holding the brakes, increasing engine speed, and shutting off one set of spark plugs using the knob above you on the left. If the engine continues to run, I'll turn that system back on and turn the second set of spark plugs off. If the engine continues to run, we'll have proven that both systems are alive and well. Then I'll confirm that both magnetos are in the on position, and we'll check our instruments for proper oil pressure and temperature, and, last, we'll make sure the controls move freely."

Jake ran through the run-up point by point. Kate had to look up at the left wing root to see the magneto switch, and move her knees apart to allow the stick to move around without hitting them. "Okay, missy, look around and see if there are any planes coming into land."

"I don't see anything in the sky," she replied, craning her neck this way and that. Jake increased the engine speed and released the brakes, guiding the yellow Cub onto the runway and aligning it with the center line. "All set?"

"Just one moment, Mr. Jake," Kate said as she sat in the front seat looking through the spinning propeller. After a long moment, Kate finally spoke up. "Okay, all set!"

"Anything wrong?"

"No, I just wanted to savor the moment," the girl replied.

Jake smiled and advanced the throttle.

Kate felt the aircraft come alive as the noise, vibration, and wind increased. As the aircraft accelerated down the runway, she could feel the flight controls take effect when Jake pushed forward on the stick, raising the tail and lowering the nose, allowing Kate to see the runway rushing under them. She felt the back of the plane moving side to side as Jake steered with the rudder while balancing the now nimble craft on the main gear. Kate stared straight ahead taking in the noise, the vibrations, and the rush of scenery. And then they were up! Kate felt the smoothness of the air and watched the shadow of the plane cast from the late-day sun move away and grow smaller.

"How are we doing up there, missy?"

"This is wonderful, everything looks so beautiful!" Kate replied, as she looked intently over the nose. She thrilled to feel the plane accelerate as it climbed above the trees at the far end of the runway.

It surged up for a brief moment, as if it had hit a soft bump. *I can feel the air holding us up*, she thought as she watched everything get smaller.

"We have a perfect evening; the air is nice and smooth, so just sit back and enjoy the ride."

"How high are we going?"

"Well, I think everything looks so much prettier down low, so let's stay at seven hundred feet for a while, then we'll climb above the hills to the east and see if there are any hot air balloons flying tonight."

The yellow Cub rose at a steady rate into the clear, smooth evening air. "I can see the Malt Shop," Kate noted. "And out by that hill—I think that's my uncle's vineyard. Mr. Jake, can we fly over there?"

"We certainly can, missy." Jake banked the plane to the left and followed the main road toward Frank Wilson's place. It all made sense to Kate—the Malt Shop, the main road, and her uncle's vineyard up ahead. Kate followed their progress as if reading a map, knowing right where she was. However, a few things didn't seem to make sense to her, and one vineyard seemed out of place until she saw the red pickup truck that Bruce and his mother had driven to the fair. Like magic, she was able to recognize all of the buildings and ponds.

As they flew closer, Kate could not believe her luck, for down below, Bruce Gillman was loading the back of the pickup. "Mr. Jake, do you see that red truck down there? Can we circle it? That's my friend Bruce!"

Jake took a moment to pick out the vehicle, then banked the Cub smartly over on its left wing. "Wow," Kate gasped, grabbing the sides of the cockpit. "Can we crash if you tilt over that far?"

"Not if it's done correctly, missy. I'm sorry I startled you. I'll give you a warning next time. Let's circle around until he looks up, then I'll rock the wings so he knows it's you."

Down below, Bruce had just finished loading the truck with bags of lime when he heard a small plane. Not thinking anything about it, he walked around to get into the driver's seat. Although Bruce was not old enough to drive on county roads, he, like so many other young men and women, operated machinery on farms and vineyards starting at an early age. As he reached the driver's side door, Bruce finally took note that the plane overhead was not departing as quickly as most did. Looking toward the sound, Bruce was blinded by the sun and raised a hand to shield his eyes from the glare. Then from behind his outstretched hand, a small plane appeared moving right to left, its yellow color becoming more obvious each second it moved further away from the sun. Bruce knew in an instant why the plane was circling. It was Kate taking her airplane ride, and now the wings of the plane were rocking! Bruce snatched the hat from his head and waved with wide sweeps of his hand and a big smile. *How cool is that!* he thought as he continued to wave.

The Cub made three orbits before departing to the south, but not before Bruce made out a small arm sticking out of the plane, waving. Bruce smiled to himself. "Looks like she's having a good time."

In the plane, Kate was so thrilled that Bruce had seen them and waved that she looked back over her shoulder and gave Jake a thumbs-up, her smile lighting her face. Jake smiled, happy Kate was enjoying the flight.

The yellow Cub continued south toward Frank's vineyard. Of course, Frank and Sue were waiting back at the airport so there was no one to wave at, but Kate wanted to circle the place, anyway. By this time Jake was taking his cues from just watching Kate, and he put the

Cub into a gentle bank above the vineyard as the girl took it all in. There below her was the farmhouse, the dirt road leading to the vineyard, and the tractor sitting right where she had left it. She also saw the field she had just cut that afternoon and again wondered if a small plane could actually land on it.

"Look to the east, missy, just past the ridge. Do you see them?" Jake asked.

"Yes, I do," Kate responded. "Hot air balloons, just like you said. Can we get closer?"

"Sure we can," Jake assured her as he leveled off on an easterly heading. "Kate, why don't you put your feet on the rudder pedals and your right hand on the stick so you can fly for a while."

"Okay," Kate replied in a less than enthusiastic voice.

"Look, missy, I'm right here and I won't let anything happen to you. Remember, move the stick side to side to keep the wings level or bank, and pull or push the stick slowly to raise or lower the nose. And the rudder is used..."

"To counteract adverse yaw," Kate quickly finished, remembering what Jake had taught her when they first met.

"Okay, missy, give it a try. Just keep the wings level and the nose sitting right where it is on the horizon. Remember, small corrections."

Kate took hold of the stick, at first afraid to move it. Slowly she added a bit of back pressure needed to hold the nose from going down and then started making small

83

corrections as the airplane proceeded east, toward the two hot air balloons. Her confidence grew as she got a feel for the controls and realized that the airplane needed little input from the pilot to fly straight and level in such smooth air.

"See, you're doing great now. Let's try a turn to the left. First look behind you to the left to see if there are any airplanes around, then feed in some left stick to start the plane banking to the left, then a bit of left rudder. You'll have to pull a little, or increase back pressure, on the stick to prevent the nose from going down as the plane turns."

Kate followed Jake's instructions and banked the Cub to the left. "That's it, missy. Now, once the plane is banked, you bring the stick back to center and just give it what it needs to remain in the turn. Glance at the black ball in the liquid-filled glass tube in front of you. See how the glass tube looks like a smiley face? We want that black ball to stay right in the middle between those two lines. If the ball moves to the left of the tube, add some left rudder; that ball tells if you're pointed directly into the airflow. We call that coordinated flight. It's easy to know what rudder to use to move the ball back into its cage, just remember to 'step on the ball.'"

Jake allowed Kate to make a full turn before taking back control and continuing toward their target.

With Jake flying, Kate was able to watch the multicolored balloons, brilliantly lit by the low sun. She was thrilled to see the people in the baskets wave as the Cub turned west.

"We'll head back to the airport now, missy. How

about you take the controls again and I'll talk you into the pattern."

"I don't want to land the plane," Kate protested.

"Okay, but you can get us into the traffic pattern. I promise I will take over after you have us aimed at the runway."

"All right, Mr. Jake. I'll give it a try as long as you talk me through it."

Jake sat quietly as Kate piloted the small craft back toward the airport, giving her an opportunity to really get the feel of flying a small plane.

As she flew, Kate looked around. There was so much to take in as the small craft continued on. Kate began to appreciate the antique instruments in front of her, the fabric covering the sides of the cockpit, and the tubing. Not that it looked old, just not at all what she had expected. And the engine purred along as if not working hard at all. Then there was that strange-looking wire, sticking straight up just a few inches in front of the windshield, which seemed to bob up and down. "Mr. Jake, what is that wire in front of me that keeps moving?"

Jake chuckled. "That's the fuel gauge. You see, the fuel tank sits in front of the instrument panel, the rod sticking out of the fuel cap is connected to a float in the tank. As the fuel is used up, the rod gets shorter and shorter. Real simple."

"Wow, that's amazing," Kate replied, shaking her head. Then she announced nervously, "I see the airport."

"Okay, missy, I want you to head for the end of the runway with the number one painted on it. I'll tell you when I want you to make a right turn and fly parallel to the runway. We'll call this the downwind leg."

As the Cub approached the airport, Jake talked Kate through the turn to downwind. "Kate, now I'm going to reduce power so we can slow up a bit. You keep adding back pressure on the stick so the plane holds this altitude. I want you to look at the airspeed indicator and turn the trim crank handle on your left counterclockwise until there is no pressure on the stick at fifty-five miles per hour. The ship will start to descend on its own; you make sure we hold fifty-five."

Kate made the control inputs as requested, first slowing down and then holding fifty-five.

"Good job, Kate. Raise the nose to slow down, lower the nose to speed up."

Kate felt they were flying too far past the runway when Jake spoke up. "Now start another ninety-degree turn to the left, keeping that ball in the center. We call this the base leg. Keep shifting your gaze between the airspeed indicator and the runway."

The plane was a half mile from the runway, and only a few hundred feet in the air, its flight path at a right angle to the long strip of asphalt. Kate waited for the command to turn, totally consumed by concentration. "Excellent, Kate, now start your turn, so we level out looking straight down the runway."

Kate banked to the left, having a hard time keeping the ball in the middle, then felt Jake on the controls for a moment, getting everything back in shape. "That's it, missy—we're all lined up, I'll take it from here. Hey, you did great!"

On the ground, Frank and Sue watched intently as the small craft approached the airport. Sue had her phone to her ear, giving Anna a blow-by-blow description of what was happening. Lined up with the runway, the yellow Cub looked nostalgic, echoing what was probably an everyday occurrence back in the 1930s and '40s.

"I hope she had a good experience," Sue told Anna as the plane leveled off a foot above the runway and settled down for a perfect landing. "And they're down."

Frank and Susan watched as the Cub sort of waddled off the runway and taxied up to the hangar, stopping frequently, sort of feeling its way as it turned in between the two buildings. The engine noise ceased as the beautiful wood propeller slowed to a stop, then there was quiet...for a moment.

"That was *great!*" Kate yelled, throwing her hands in the air as if scoring the winning point in a sports competition. "I flew an airplane!"

Jake, surprised by Kate's enthusiasm, looked down smiling to himself.

Frank came over and helped Kate get out of the plane, as Sue ended her call with Anna and snapped pictures. Jake came around the strut to shake Kate's hand but instead got a big hug!

"Thank you, Mr. Jake! That was the most exciting thing I have ever done. Uncle Frank, we saw Bruce, we rocked our wings, and he saw us and waved back. Then we circled two hot air balloons and I flew the plane. That was me in the landing pattern!"

"Fantastic, Kate! We were hoping you liked it."

"I loved it, Uncle Frank. You can see for miles and miles, the world looked like a train set."

"Kate, stand next to Jake, I want to take a picture," Sue directed as she snapped away.

"Jake, how can we help you get things put away?" Frank asked.

"I'll tell you what. If the two of you push on the struts, I'll guide the tail, and tell you when to stop pushing."

With the plane back in the hangar, Frank again thanked Jake for his kindness. "Oh, believe me, Frank, it was no bother. Kate picks things up quickly, she'd make a great pilot."

Kate was still beaming. "Thank you, Mr. Jake."

"Kate, if you'd like, we can do this again in a few weeks, if it's all right with your parents."

"I would love that, thank you."

"You're welcome, missy." Jake turned to Kate's uncle. "Frank, before you go, I want to give you an application for something called a Young Eagles ride. The program is run by the Experimental Aircraft Association, or EAA. It's a great program and there's a lot more to it than just an airplane ride."

"Experimental aircraft...so NASA experiments with Piper Cubs or something?" Frank asked, hoping Jake was kidding.

Jake laughed, never having heard it put like that before. "No, Frank, 'experimental' is just the category the FAA gives aircraft that are not built in factories. People all over the world build their own planes, and the EAA represents many of them. I have an application in the hangar that will explain what the Young Eagles program is, and what the EAA is all about. If you can, send it off to Kate's parents and have them sign it and send it back. We can make Kate's second ride an official Young Eagles ride."

"I'm looking forward to learning more about this, Jake; I'll get it in the mail tomorrow, thanks," Frank ended, again shaking Jake's hand.

Daylight was fading from the sky as Jake pulled into the diner. Walking in Jake nodded to Lynn, who grabbed a menu and followed him to a table.

"How are you this evening, Jake?" she asked, handing him the menu.

"Oh, I don't need to look at that, I'll have the meatloaf and unsweetened iced tea."

"Sure thing, Jake," Lynn replied.

Lynn returned a minute later with iced tea and placed it on the table, then sat down next to a surprised Jake and looked him square in the eye.

"Listen, tough guy, I don't know if you have to be hit over the head with a two-by-four before you realize that Chris has a crush on you. She's a real nice girl and I know for a fact that she would say yes if you asked her out to dinner...as long as you're not planning on taking her here for dinner, that is."

Then, before Jake had a chance to react, Lynn got up and walked away. Jake was perplexed for a few moments, his first thought being *What the heck does Chris see in me?* and his second thought being *I'm hungry, where's that meatloaf?*

Kate had trouble falling to sleep that night as she replayed the week's events over and over in her head. She thought about the fair with Bruce, and him waving as she flew overhead. Then her thoughts turned to home and her friends. After a while, exhaustion won out and Kate drifted off. Her last thoughts were of...

Downstairs, Frank and Sue were getting ready to turn in for the night, after finishing her call with Anna and Bob. Frank locked up while Sue turned off lights in the kitchen. In the bedroom, Sue stopped and looked at her husband, who was sitting on the edge of their bed deep in thought. "What?"

"I keep thinking that Jake and I have met before."

Sue laughed. "You probably have, honey, it's a small valley."

Frank shrugged and shut off the lights.

Chapter 9:
The Second Flight

Sparkling sunlight lit Kate's auburn hair as it tossed about, blasted by the wind coming in through the half window of the Cub, and at five thousand feet and seventy-five miles per hour, there was quite a bit of wind. Kate had spent the time leading up to this second flight working around the vineyard, bowling with Bruce, and going to the movies, where she had a chance to meet some of Bruce's friends. Afterward everyone went for dessert at the ice cream shop, where Kate explained from the back deck how she had seen Jake's plane as it approached the airport.

Now it was mid-August, and once again Kate was airborne, sitting in the front seat of Jake's vintage aircraft. Only this time they were much higher.

"Okay, Kate, let me take it for a while. I want to demonstrate what happens when you fly too slow," Jake said as he gave the stick a short shake side to side, confirming that he had it. Kate let go of the stick and sat almost motionless in the front seat waiting for the *dreaded stall* that Jake had described on the ground. Actually, Kate added the word *dreaded*. Jake just called it an aerodynamic stall, describing what happened when a wing sliced the air at too great an angle, which caused airflow attached to the top of the wing to separate. Until then this flight had been just as magical as the first flight a few weeks before. This time Jake had taken the tiny Cub a mile into the sky, allowing Kate to view the entire Napa Valley. She could even see the Pacific Ocean, shrouded by fog banks just offshore, and the Golden Gate Bridge far to the south.

"Okay, I'm going to bring the throttle to idle. Then, as the plane slows down, instead of lowering the nose to hold our best glide speed, I'm going to keep pulling back on the stick, raising the nose, trying to keep us at the same altitude. This is something a pilot might mistakenly do trying to stretch a glide after an engine failure."

"Mr. Jake, I'm kind of scared," Kate confessed, immediately regretting her statement. Would Jake think she was a sissy, or maybe cut the flight short and give up on the little scaredy-cat in the front seat?

"Hey, kiddo, it's about time you called me Jake, and not Mr. Jake. Nothing to be afraid of, missy. As soon as the stall breaks, we'll release back pressure on the stick to lower the nose and get the air flowing over the wings again, and add power before bringing the nose back up to the horizon. Are you ready?"

Gee, Kate thought. *Jake would make anyone feel comfortable.* "Okay, Jake," she replied, feeling very grown-up dropping the "mister."

"Okay, Kate, keep your eye on the airspeed indicator and the attitude of the airplane." Jake brought the throttle to idle and waited as the craft slowed. Kate sat transfixed as the engine roar subsided and the blast of wind turned into a breeze. The seasoned pilot eased the stick back further and further, keeping the Cub at the same altitude as it slowed, forcing the wings to slice into the oncoming air at greater and greater angles. Kate grabbed the two support tubes in front of her as the plane began to buffet as the wings stalled, causing her to yelp as she watched the nose fall through the horizon.

Kate felt it in her stomach as the nose dropped,

before pulling up in response to Jake's inputs as the Cub returned to straight and level flight. Her relief was immediate.

"Wow, that was awesome, Jake, but what's so dangerous about a stall? It didn't seem like such a big deal."

"Oh no, look at the altimeter Kate, we lost...no, we fell over one hundred feet! If that happened in the traffic pattern or while maneuvering near the ground, we would have been in big trouble. And sloppy flying could cause one wing to stall more than the other, causing the ship to go into a spin. That's why it's so important to learn how to recognize and recover from a stall, or, better yet, never let a situation develop that might lead to a stall. Oh, and you were right expressing your apprehension, Kate. When you're alone up here, that little voice in your head will tell you when something is not a good idea. Now would you like to try one?"

Far below, Kate's parents craned their necks searching the crystal-clear sky, guided only by the faint sound of an aircraft engine. Unbeknown to their daughter, the two parents had driven up to Napa to surprise Kate after having spent the preceding day visiting Carmel on a brief but needed getaway. The plan was to surprise Kate before her flight, but traffic had held them up. Sue ended up driving her niece to the airport, not telling Kate about her parents' visit. Now, after just arriving at Frank's vineyard, the weary travelers scanned the sky looking for the small yellow plane as they waited for Frank to retrieve a pair of binoculars.

"Found them," Frank announced, spotting the Cub through the binoculars after running out of the house. He handed the binoculars to Bob, who peered toward the faint drone coming from the sky. "There, I see it—yep, it's a Cub, all right. I thought you told me they fly around only a few hundred feet up."

"Well, that's what they did on their first flight, I guess they're doing something different today. Must be a hell of a view."

Sue, who had just returned from the airport, parked the pickup and joined everyone looking at the sky. "I can't believe they're that high!" Anna lamented.

Sue gave Anna a hug. "I'm sure they're fine and having a great time. Now come on inside and freshen up before we head to the airport."

Meanwhile, Jake suggested, "Kate, let's head off to the east and burn off some of this altitude."

Kate peered over her left shoulder looking for other aircraft before putting the Cub into a gradual left bank. After she leveled off, Jake gave the stick a shake. "I've got it, Kate. I want to show you something about making steep turns."

When sure Kate had released control, Jake continued, "In level flight, we feel the normal pull of

94

gravity expressed as one g. As we make a turn, the wing has to hold us up and change our direction. As it does, we feel an increase in weight, or g-force, as our bodies are forced to change direction. At a sixty-degree bank, we feel twice as heavy, or we're pulling two g. If you're up to it, I'll demonstrate a tight turn, so you can experience what this feels like."

Kate had already felt the sensation of being pushed into her seat while they were maneuvering, but Jake was going to show her something a little more intense.

Kate gave him a thumbs-up, so Jake, after looking over his shoulder, put the Cub into a tight bank. Kate sank in her seat as she looked at the low wing, amazed that it was pointing at the same spot on the ground as the world spun, as if it was a record spinning on a turntable. Jake finally leveled the plane on its original heading. "Well, Kate, do you think you can handle one of those?"

"That was intense. I felt so heavy. What do I do if I can't control it?"

"Level the wings, ball centered, and recover gently to level flight. Don't worry Kate, I'm right here."

Kate looked around for other aircraft then banked the Cub. Further and further…forty-five, fifty degrees…keeping the ball centered. She was surprised by how hard she had to pull on the stick to keep the plane's nose level with the horizon, finally adding opposite aileron to stop the ever-increasing bank. Around she went, working against the force of gravity.

"Okay, bring her back to level," Jake instructed as the plane completed a full turn.

"That wasn't bad for your first try, Kate. Let's take a break and just fly straight. We'll lose some altitude and then head to the airport with the sun at our back."

"That sounds like a good idea, Jake. That turn made me a little dizzy."

"Believe me, you'll get used to it, but you do have to build up a resistance. I'll fly until you feel better, just sit back and enjoy the ride."

The pair flew east, slowly descending until at seven hundred feet Jake turned west. Kate was having the time of her life.

"We can go a little lower out here, there are no houses or people," Jake said as he reduced power and descended to a mere two hundred feet above the ground. At this altitude, Kate felt as if she was flying on a magic carpet. Details of the landscape were easier to make out, as the plane's path matched the contour of the hills. Jake slowed the aircraft further, allowing the scenery to pass under the wings at a more leisurely pace. Kate sat there taking everything in, the beauty of the landscape, the gentle breeze, and the smell of fresh-cut hay from the farm below. Jake made a sweeping right turn to avoid a small town and remained over open farmland as their tour continued.

When he added full power, the Cub climbed back up to one thousand feet and leveled off.

"Okay, missy, the airport is five miles up ahead, and I want you to bring us in. We'll be coming in from the east again; you already know what that looks like, so let's review what the plan is."

96

Kate sat up straight to indicate she was ready.

"Okay," Jake continued. "The airport elevation is ninety feet above sea level, so we need one thousand ninety feet on the altimeter to enter the pattern at one thousand. You'll be making a right turn into the downwind leg about a half mile out, flying parallel with the runway. You're going to put on carburetor heat—that's the knob on the right—so let's pull it out about halfway. It directs heated air to the carburetor, keeping it from icing up."

Kate looked down and touched the knob marked "Carburetor Heat."

"When we're adjacent to our touchdown point, bring the throttle back to idle and start raising the nose to hold altitude as we slow down to fifty-five. Then you can lower the nose a bit and trim the aircraft as you did on the first flight, to hold that speed. I'll tell you when to make the left onto the base leg; you're going to decide when to make your left turn to final, and line up with the runway. Remember to hold fifty-five and make a nice coordinated turn. That means keeping the ball centered."

"Why didn't we use carb heat last time?"

"We did, but you had enough to think about so I put it on."

Kate's heart beat faster in anticipation, now that she knew what a stall was and that accurate airspeed control was essential.

"Okay, Kate, left hand on the throttle and hold seventy. You see the airport in front of us, now begin your right turn."

Kate moved the stick to the right, adding a bit of

right rudder. She instinctively added back pressure to keep the nose from dipping and held the plane in the turn until they were flying parallel to, and about a half mile from, the runway.

"Very nice, missy, now put on your carb heat."

Kate verified and pulled the knob out halfway.

"Okay, you remember where we touched down the other day. I want you to reduce power to idle when we're abreast that point, and increase back pressure to hold altitude and start slowing down."

Kate felt every fiber of her body concentrating on following Jake's instructions. She moved the throttle back to idle, keeping her hand on it in case she needed power. It took more effort than she expected to hold the plane's nose up as the speed decreased. Jake reminded her to crank in some nose-up trim. "The crank handle on the right side of the cockpit—crank it counterclockwise to reduce the pressure you need to hold the nose up."

Kate cranked until the stick needed no pressure to maintain fifty-five miles per hour, and studied the airport as she flew past the end of the runway.

"All right, Kate, start your ninety-degree left turn onto the base leg, and keep a lookout for other airplanes."

Lower and lower the Cub descended, Kate's eyes darting from the runway off to her left and the airspeed indicator.

"Very nice, Kate. Look to the right and make sure no aircraft are on a long final approach. You're doing great, missy. Speed at fifty-five, now decide when to turn final to line up with the runway."

Kate's mind raced to keep up as a small bump upset the aircraft. Holding the plane steady, she began the turn early but on recognizing it opened the turn until the Cub was headed straight at the runway. "Outstanding, Kate, very good. Now pay attention to your touchdown point and aim about one hundred feet in front of it. That point should remain stationary in the windshield as it grows larger. If it appears to rise in the windshield, we're getting low and need a bit of power. Don't raise the nose, just add power. If the touchdown point appears to be going down in the windshield, we're high, in which case we'll just land further down the runway. Now I want you to head for the grass off to the right—you're going to land the plane."

"What!"

"Just do what I say, missy, we'll do it together." Jake gave the stick a slight wiggle to prove he was with her. "We're going to continue like this right down until we are just a bit lower than the treetops. Then I want you to look out to the other end of the runway and raise the nose until the panel is even with the end of the airport, and level out just above the grass. The nose will be in your way, so just look off to the side of the nose until she touches down, then stick all the way back and hold it there as we roll out. Remember to use the rudder to keep it rolling straight with quick jabs."

Kate didn't answer, opting to give the stick a shake. On the ground, Kate's parents had arrived just in time to see the small yellow plane approach the pattern.

Kate's mind raced as she kept glancing at the

airspeed indicator, then back out toward the runway. It looked good, but as they descended, the touchdown point appeared to rise.

"A little power Kate. That's it, not too much."

"Okay, missy, here we go...look down to the other end and start leveling off...that's it...hold the nose there...great, now hold it off."

Kate strained to look over the nose, then remembered to look off to the sides. For a long moment, the plane seemed to just glide along the grass, neither sinking nor rising.

"Don't let it touch, Kate...bring the nose up...hold it there."

Kate felt the tires touch for a moment, then take the plane's full weight. But it wasn't over. The plane bounced a few times as it rolled out, the tail wheel finally adding to the vibrations.

"Okay, stick back in your belly," Jake reminded, as he helped Kate use the rudder to steer the bouncing craft along the not-so-smooth turf before rolling to a stop. "You did it, Kate. That was all you!"

"Wow—that was amazing! Oh my God, I don't think I took a breath. Holy mackerel, I landed!"

"Great job, missy. Now push in the carb heat to off and let's head for the hangar."

Bob and Anna looked at each other. "Do you think she was flying?"

"I don't know," Bob answered, looking at his brother and Sue for input. Frank just stood there shaking his head. "I don't know if she was flying, but it sure looked like it. We'll just have to wait a few more moments and ask."

Everyone watched as the Piper Cub taxied up and came to a stop. Kate was concentrating so hard on keeping the Cub on the taxiway that she didn't even see her parents standing by the hangar. A moment later, the engine stopped, and the propeller came to a halt.

Kate, looking toward the hangar, could not believe what she saw. "Mom, Dad—you're here! Did you see me? I landed!" Kate yelled, tears gushing from her eyes as she undid her belts and removed her headset.

Frank gave Jake a thumbs-up as the pilot sat there with a big grin, taking it all in, as Kate scrambled from the cockpit and ran to her mother and father. "I missed you both so much!" she said, crying as she hugged both of them. "Dad, I flew the plane! Did you see me land?"

"Kate, somehow I knew it was you landing," Bob said, laughing.

"Sweetheart, you did wonderfully, we're so proud of you," Anna added, wiping away tears.

"Bob, Anna, I'd like to introduce Jake Hollerman," Frank interrupted, as Jake walked out from under the wing. Bob separated himself from the women and shook Jake's hand. "Jake, I can't thank you enough for taking an interest in our daughter's newfound infatuation with airplanes."

"Bob, it's my pleasure. Sue dropped off the signed Young Eagles application, so this was Kate's official Young Eagles flight. I have to tell you, she has a real natural ability. You know that was her landing back there."

101

"She's a good kid, and I think you made a big impression on her. Thank you, you're a good man."

"Don't say that to anyone over at the diner; the girls will start expecting me to smile," Jake interjected, making everyone laugh. "Frank just told me that you're here to take Kate back to LA...?"

"That's right. School starts soon, and we thought we would spend a few days seeing the local sights with Kate before the school year starts."

Kate, hearing this for the first time, grabbed her mother's arm. "Is that right, Mom?"

"Yes, dear, we wanted to surprise you, and I just plain missed you. Is that all right?"

"Of course, it is. I missed you so much." Then Kate realized that this would be the last time she would fly with Jake, and spun around to look at him.

"So, Kate," he said, "am I going to see you next summer?"

"If my aunt and uncle will have me," Kate said, looking back at Sue.

"Nothing would make us happier, honey," Sue replied with a smile.

Jake walked Bob a few steps away from everyone and said in a hushed voice, "Bob, with your permission, I'd like to give Kate a book to study. It's a basic flight manual written many years ago, and although it's out of date, the book is a wonderful introduction to the art of flying."

"Jake, that's nice of you, but you'll have to be patient with her. She is a very slow reader, something we've been trying to work on. Unfortunately, getting Kate

102

to read anything is like pulling teeth."

Jake looked down for a moment, then over toward Kate.

"Well, she picks things up fast, and she seemed enthusiastic when we were up there. If she wants to pursue this, she's going to have to put in the time and effort. There is a lot of studying that goes into flying."

"I'll tell you what," Bob said, looking over at his daughter. "Why don't we leave it up to her."

Jake walked over. "Kate, I'd like to talk with you a moment, and I have a book that I'd like you to have."

"Mom, I'll be right back," Kate called over her shoulder, feeling very grown-up as she followed Jake into the hangar.

Jake walked to the back of the hangar and removed a book from his file cabinet. "Kate, I don't usually go into so much detail with Young Eagles, but I made you the exception because of your enthusiasm. The question is, would you like to take flying lessons next year?"

Kate thought for a moment, surprised by Jake's serious demeanor. "I have to ask my father."

Jake smiled. "I already did, and he's leaving the decision up to you."

"Gee, I don't think I would ever be smart enough to actually be a pilot, Jake. I don't know."

"Listen to me, missy, you're much smarter than you give yourself credit for. I'm not saying it's easy, but I'm impressed by how quickly you've picked things up. I think you're a natural. The book is a basic flight manual, so here's the deal. If you take it, you're making a commitment to me, to know what's in it by next summer. I'm not even going to hand it to you now; you think about it. I'm going to put it on the table and walk out of here. I'll wait for you outside."

With that, Jake walked toward the open hangar, placing the book on the table as he passed.

Kate hesitated, afraid of making a commitment she didn't think she could live up to. She looked at the Cub, remembering the awe she felt the day she walked up to it, and the exhilaration she felt after landing. Kate walked over to the table, again looked back at the Cub, as a breeze blew into the open hangar. She knew Jake was right; she would love to learn how to fly. She just doubted herself.

Kate picked up the book, *Stick and Rudder*, and walked out of the hangar.

#

Frank and Susan pulled up to their house with Bob, Anna, and Kate close behind. Kate closed the book and followed everyone to the house.

"That was a fantastic day," Frank reflected as everyone gathered on the porch. "Kate, after lunch, can you finish up the last of your chores before leaving tomorrow? It should take less than an hour. What do you say, kiddo—want to show Mom and Dad what you've been up to all summer?"

Kate grinned. "Sure thing, Uncle Frank!"

Sue also smiled, opening the screen door. "All right, everyone, I have sandwiches and iced tea in the kitchen."

Anna figured something was up by the smile on her

daughter's face and spent lunch trying to guess what those chores were.

Kate finished eating in minutes and jumped up. "I'll be back in a minute, Dad," giving him a kiss on the cheek before running up to her room. Bob gave a suspicious look to his brother, who only shrugged. Kate changed into her coveralls, scuffed-up work boots, baseball hat, and dirty work gloves and came down the stairs, walking right past her parents, who looked at each other and hurriedly followed her outside. Kate climbed onto the tractor, started it up, and drove off toward the lower field.

Again Bob and Anna looked at each other, then looked at Frank, before again watching in disbelief as their little girl drove the enormous machine down the dirt road before disappearing around the bend.

"Frank, we don't let her take out the garbage; I can't believe you trust her to drive that thing."

"And how did you convince her to wear those work clothes?" Anna added, looking at her sister-in-law.

Frank said seriously, "You'd be surprised what your daughter is capable of, Bob. She's going to attach a mower to the back of that thing and mow the last few acres of grass in the lower field. She's been doing it all summer and doing a great job of it; you should be proud of her."

Sue nodded her head in agreement. Anna, whose eyes had welled up with tears again, went over and hugged Frank. "Thank you, Frank," was all she could get out. Bob just stood there, shaking his head. "I'll be damned," he uttered as he gave Sue a hug.

The four adults decided to walk off lunch by

walking to the fields Kate was mowing. Bob and Anna watched as their not-so-little girl rode back and forth—on a tractor, of all things.

Kate turned the tractor toward her family after cutting the last strip of grass, shut it down, and jumped off in front of her parents.

"I can't believe you're driving that thing!" Anna exclaimed. "How on earth did you keep this a secret all these weeks?"

"It was hard not to slip, Mom, but I wanted it to be a surprise. Uncle Frank taught me how to drive it right after you left, then a week later, he dropped me off next to the tractor, told me not to hit anything, and just drove away, leaving me there to cut the field. Mom, I was scared to death, but I did it!"

"And that's the day Kate first saw Jake's plane," Frank added.

"I'm proud of you, sweetheart, but I'm mad at your uncle," Bob said, looking in Frank's direction. "Now instead of a car you're gonna want me to buy you a tractor!" Everyone burst out laughing.

"Oh, and I forgot to tell everyone, we have a special treat for the two of you after dinner," Sue announced, "and it's Kate's favorite place."

Leaving the tractor where it was, Kate held her father's hand as she joined her mother, aunt, and uncle for the walk back to the house. She felt proud of herself, taking stock of how much she had matured. No longer a little girl, she was now, as her father said, a "young woman who could drive a tractor and fly!"

106

Indeed, much had changed that summer, but right then as she held her father's hand, she was still daddy's little girl.

#

That evening at Clearview Airport, Jake pushed his trusty steed back into the hangar as darkness began to fall. After Kate and her family left, Jake had lunch, then flew out to the high country to the east, landing on a vacant hilltop, and sat next to the plane just enjoying the view of the valley below, and the solitude of his surroundings. He couldn't help but think of his daughter, Mary, and how happy Kate had been in the air and after landing. If only he could have seen the same joy in his daughter's eyes.

Jake looked down, wiping away tears.

The trip back in smooth air was the perfect setting for a Cub. Low and slow, the tiny plane sailed above the countryside, the long shadows accentuating hills and valleys, affording views beyond compare. As the small yellow plane descended toward the airport that evening, Jake missed seeing a young girl frantically waving from the deck of the ice cream parlor.

Chapter 10:
Home Again

The two vacation weeks Kate spent with her mom and dad seemed to go by in a flash. After leaving the vineyard, they traveled to Muir Woods to see the redwoods, spent some time with old neighbors in Fremont, and visited the aquarium at Monterey Bay. Texting with Jess on the way home, Kate kept getting the feeling that Jess was being evasive about her weekend. Kate and Jess had talked often during the trip, and Kate couldn't wait to see her friend.

The Wilsons got home past midnight, tired but happy to be back. The next morning, Kate finished unpacking and finally got a chance to call Jess, agreeing to meet on the bench in front of the building at 10:30.

"Hi, stranger," Jess yelled as she came down the front steps.

"Hi, friend," Kate answered as both girls hugged. Kate and Jess talked for over an hour about each other's summer, with Jess asking most of the questions. Toward the end of their conversation, Kate finally asked about the weekend.

"Jess, I know you said you were going to visit your cousin Vicky the other day, but you never told me how she was, or what the two of you did."

Jess looked down and paused, then took Kate's hand.

"Vicky is great. We went to Hermosa Beach and took a nice long walk along the Strand." Again Jess paused. "Kate, I saw Tony."

Kate stared at Jess. "Did you talk to him?"

"Yes, but only for a minute. He was hanging out with three other boys and a man. I asked him how he was. He just shrugged. Then I asked him what school he was going to go to, and he didn't even know the name. I don't think he cares. It was strange."

Jess stopped, because what she was about to say was going to hurt her friend. "Kate, Tony said he didn't remember you."

Kate was taken aback. She never expected that; she'd thought she meant something to Tony.

Jess squeezed her friend's hand. "I didn't know if I should tell you, but I figured you had a right to know. I know you liked him."

It took a minute, but Kate finally looked at Jess. "It's okay, honey, it's okay. That's in the past. I didn't think the rumors were true about him, but you were right all along." Kate looked out toward the park, as memories of the evening came flooding back when it dawned on her. The plane! That beautiful blue and yellow plane, that's why I was so excited seeing Jake's Cub in the sky that day.

Kate stopped and smiled as her demeanor changed. "Come on, Jess, let's go upstairs. I want to show you pictures I took last week, and I have a new picture of Bruce!"

# # #

Kate's sophomore year was well underway keeping

her busier than ever. There were so many things she had to do, and being on the swim team just added to the demands on her time. Not that she didn't enjoy swimming or her teammates, it just took time.

Late one afternoon, Kate was listening to music, talking to friends on the phone, and texting—in fact, she had five text conversations going at once—her mother knocked on her bedroom door. "Kate," Anna said through the door. "I have something for you that came in the mail today."

Kate sprang up from her bed and opened the door.

"Have you finished your homework?" her mother asked.

"Not yet, I was just taking a break. What's for dinner?"

"Pot roast," Anna replied, handing her daughter the small box. "It's from Aunt Susan."

"Thanks, Mom!" Kate said as she inspected the box.

"Just open it, dear. I've been waiting all day to see what it is."

Kate checked her phone again before ripping open the wrapping, exposing a white rectangular box. Kate used her fingernail to cut two pieces of tape and removed the cover, revealing a silver picture frame, which she gently removed. The frame held a picture of Kate and Jake standing in front of Jake's yellow Piper Cub, taken by her aunt after Kate's first flight. Kate smiled, the same smile she wore in the picture.

"Oh, that's beautiful," Anna said, "and what a

lovely frame. I have to call Sue right now and tell her you got it, and how you smiled when you opened the box."

Anna left Kate, who stood motionless, looking at the picture. She could almost feel the wind in her hair.

After setting the picture on her bookshelf, Kate paused, remembering everything that happened during her stay at the vineyard. She wondered how Bruce's school year was going, then sat down at her computer to write to him. But her phone again beckoned, showing twelve text messages urgently waiting to be answered.

"Dinner's ready," her mother called.

"Okay, Mom," Kate answered, texting feverishly. She never looked up from her phone as she exited her bedroom and walked right into her father, who was on his way to her room to say hello, having just gotten home from work.

"Hi, Daddy," Kate said as she kissed her dad on the cheek. Bob felt a bit hurt by his daughter barely looking up from her phone.

"Kate, enough of that now, put that thing down and give your mother a hand setting the table."

Kate put the phone in her pocket. *So much going on*, she thought. After dinner, Kate returned to her room and, seeing the picture, remembered something she had promised to do. She looked around until she found the book Jake had given her, under some magazines. Kate opened the book and started reading, making a real effort to concentrate. Unfortunately, her phone seemed determined to interrupt her.

# # #

As the weeks passed and the sun made its yearly migration south, Kate continued to struggle with reading and homework. She had read the first two chapters of *Stick and Rudder*, but like with so many other things, Kate became discouraged and put the book down. On a positive note, the swim team made it to the state semifinals but was eliminated in the first round.

#

Jess rang the doorbell to apartment 6A at 5:00 p.m., which was the time she always came over to Kate's house. "Come on in, honey," greeted Anna. "How is your mom doing?"

"Everything is fine, Mrs. Wilson. My mom is great, but her only day off is Sunday and that's when we do laundry and clean."

"Well, I'm sure you're a big help."

"I try to be. The good news is my mom just started seeing someone from work, and he's really nice."

Anna's eyes lit up, a smile brightening her face. "Oh Jess, I'm so happy to hear that, I really am. Kate is in her room, why don't you go in."

Since Bob was back north attending a work conference, Kate, Jess, and Anna had a great time talking about fashion, boys, television, and anything else that came to mind.

After dessert, Kate and Jess sat on Kate's bed talking and texting on their phones, until the conversation came around to Kate's flying exploits.

"Wait," Jess interrupted. "After you told me about the plane ride over the phone, I remembered something I wanted to tell you. Did you know that Mr. Rice, the science teacher, is a pilot?"

"He is?"

"I'll bet he would love to hear about what you did this summer; you have to tell him."

"All right, I'll mention it to him tomorrow." Kate was unable to disguise her excitement.

Anna yelled in, "Jess, you wanted me to remind you when it was 9:30."

"Thanks, Mrs. Wilson, I'll be right out," Jess yelled back. "I have to go, Kate."

"Okay, Jess, I'll see you in the morning."

Chapter 11: Revelations

It had been over a month since Kate left, and Jake had spent the better part of the day at the airport. Getting hungry, he headed over to the diner for dinner.

"Well, hello, Jake," Lynn said, putting a glass of unsweetened iced tea in front of him.

"Hi, Lynn, I'll have a hamburger, French fries, and a garden salad on the side," Jake responded, taking a sip of tea.

"Coming right up. Oh and by the way, Chris told me you haven't been in for breakfast in a week."

"I know. I was helping Bill the mechanic with an annual inspection, and he insisted on ordering in, but I'll be in tomorrow."

"Don't worry, honey, my lips are sealed," Lynn replied, never looking up from her order pad, then she sat across from Jake and looked him square in the eye. "Now listen, hotshot, the two of you are acting like schoolchildren, smiling at each other, a wink here and there. It's time you ask the girl out!"

With that, Lynn stood up, spun, and hastened away to place the order. Jake took a deep breath in resignation. "Well, looks like tomorrow I make a fool of myself."

Lynn returned a few minutes later with Jake's dinner. "All you tough guys are such puppies at heart. Trust me, she likes you." Lynn patted Jake on his shoulder.

114

"All right, Lynn, get out of here before the only tip you get is 'Don't smoke,'" Jake threatened as he stood to chase her away.

Lynn laughed and walked back into the kitchen, where she promptly grabbed her cell phone.

After dinner, Jake took his bill to the register, only to find Lynn standing behind the counter with a big smile on her face. "You are coming in for breakfast tomorrow, right?" she asked."

"Stop looking at me with that silly grin and give me my change," Jake responded in his best fake snarl. Suddenly he understood.

"You called her, didn't you!"

Lynn couldn't contain herself and broke out laughing. "The two of you are going to make such a cute couple."

Jake just shook his head and walked out. "Well, tomorrow I better make sure I shave."

# # #

Chris looked nervously out the window of the diner, then looked at her watch: 7:30. *He probably chickened out*, she thought as she hurriedly delivered breakfast to three impatient customers before returning to the kitchen for the bacon missing from one of the orders.

When Jake entered the diner, one of the three stood and waved.

"Jake, over here, buddy. How the hell are you!"

Jake smiled and walked over. "Still alive and kicking, Alex, mostly kicking. How are you and where did you pick up these two knuckleheads?"

All four men laughed as Jake joined the trio a moment before Chris returned from the kitchen with the bacon, placing it on the table in front of Jake by mistake.

Chris found herself looking right at Jake before realizing her mistake, and stood there speechless.

"Good morning, beautiful, I'll take my usual breakfast if that's okay?"

Chris, being caught off guard, disappeared into the kitchen to set up Jake's order and collect herself.

After eating, Jake excused himself and caught Chris as she headed for the kitchen.

"Listen, things didn't go as I had planned this morning, I was hoping to talk to you where I normally sit. So, look, would you like to have dinner with me this evening?"

Chris smiled. "Well, it's about time you asked, Jake. I've had the dress I'm wearing on our first date picked out for a month."

Jake laughed. "I'm glad I surprised you; I'll see you later, then."

"Yes, you will," Chris answered before ducking into the kitchen to Lynn.

As Jake walked to the front door, a man he thought looked familiar stood up and introduced himself. "Jake, I'm Frank Wilson, Kate's uncle."

Jake smiled and extended a hand. "Frank, how are you, and how is Kate doing?"

"Jake, are you headed for the airport? I want to talk to you about what you said to that guy, and I want to bring you up to speed on Kate."

"Gee I don't remember what I said."

"That's okay Jake, but I'd rather talk about it at the airport, if that's where you're going."

"That's exactly where I'm headed, Frank. Follow me over there and we'll talk."

Jake had just finished opening up the hangar when Frank's pickup turned the corner and parked. "So Frank, how's your wife, ah...Sue, how is she?"

"Everyone is great. Jake, can I ask you a question?"

"Of course, Frank what is it?"

Frank hesitated, then asked, "Who's Mickey Mantle?"

At first Jake was confused, then his brow wrinkled as he looked at Frank for a long moment, not understanding how he was hearing those words again.

"I was only asked that once, how could you know?"

"I thought it was you!" Frank replied, shaking his head. "Jake, I asked you that the day you got shot down in Nam!"

Jake stood speechless.

"Jake, we had just arrived in country a week before and were airlifted into that firebase barely three hours before you showed up. Our sergeant posted two of us on the perimeter, and I'm telling you, we were scared out of our wits. We were told that anyone on the other side of the barbed wire was enemy and to start shooting. Then twenty minutes later, someone yells out in perfect English that they needed help. I didn't know what the hell to do, and I was afraid to shoot because you sounded legit. The sergeant never gave us a challenge word, and Mickey Mantle was the only thing I could come up with. When you yelled at me to get over there, I felt even stupider than I did after asking such a dumb question! Then as my buddy Andy Tibbs and I were taking you to the aid station, you told me that you were still alive and kicking, mostly kicking. You just said the same thing to your friends, and that's when I knew."

Jake's eyes filled with tears, then both men hugged. When they finally separated, both men had tears in their eyes. Over the next few hours, Jake and Frank went over every detail they could remember about their time in Vietnam. Frank eventually updated Jake on how Kate was doing in school; unfortunately, the report was not favorable.

"Well, Frank, if she is interested in anything to do with aviation, she'll have to put more effort into reading and math. I think she's a real smart kid, maybe there's a reason she's having trouble. Maybe she needs glasses or something. In the meantime, please let me know if I can help in some way."

"That's great, Jake. I'm calling Bob tonight—I can't wait to tell him how we met, he probably won't believe it, and I'll let him know that you offered to help."

Jake extended his hand to the man that didn't shoot him so many years ago. "I know how scared I was, on my first missions over there. I'm sure glad you kept your head and brought me in."

"Yeah, well, I sure didn't want to clean my rifle after you got through with it." Both men laughed and

118

hugged again. "Take care, Jake. I have to get back to the vineyard, and tell Sue about this."

"Yep, this has been a hell of a day, and it's only 9:30. See you later."

Jake went back into the hangar and sat. Reliving so many stories with Frank brought back a lot of painful memories. Jake sat for the longest time in front of his workbench staring at the wall, remembering the friends he had lost.

Chapter 12:
The EAA

Jake turned his car into the parking lot of the airport and parked among the fifteen or so other cars. Although it was already dark, Jake had not come to the airport to fly. He had come for another reason.

Jake and Chris had finally gone on a date and ever since had been seeing a lot of each other. They fell into a comfortable routine of dinner on Tuesday and Thursday evenings, and weekends together. And Jake went to the diner for breakfast every morning, which Chris loved. The two had been dating for five weeks when, during dinner, Chris started asking questions about the pilots' meeting coming up at the airport. She had overheard a few men talking about it. Jake explained that it was an EAA meeting.

"Go on," Chris encouraged.

"Well," Jake opened, "the EAA was started in the early '50s by a pilot named Paul Poberezny and a small group of friends from Milwaukee who were all building their own airplanes. These guys got together on a regular basis to talk about their projects, and as word spread and interest in the group grew, they decided to form the Experimental Aircraft Association with Paul at the helm. Soon homebuilders around the country began making inquiries, so Paul began publishing a monthly newsletter. It didn't take long before pilots in California asked if they could start an EAA chapter in their town. After that, chapters sprang up all around the country, and then around the world, and the rest is history. Now there are over two hundred thousand members from all over the world."

Chris was amazed that so few people knew about this, and she wanted to learn more. Then Jake mentioned that he was a past president of the EAA chapter based at Clearview Airport.

"You're going to the meeting, aren't you?" Chris asked.

Jake had taken the hint, which was why he stood in the airport parking lot, looking at the lit windows of the airport office, figuring that he was going to catch some flak for not attending meetings.

The opposite was true. Everyone was happy to see him, and his smile made it obvious that the feeling was mutual. The big event the chapter was preparing for was their annual Young Eagles rally, scheduled for the first week in November. The program offered free airplane rides to young people between the ages of eight and seventeen as a means of introducing the younger generation to general aviation. At the rally, chapter members sold hot dogs, drinks, and potato chips, and even had a flight simulator for the families to use while they waited for their child's flight to return. Jake offered to use his plane for the rally after hearing that a plane the chapter relied on was out of the state. He even volunteered Chris to help out with registrations, hoping she would have the day off.

The next morning before sitting down for breakfast

at the diner, Jake broke the news to Chris.

"That's great, Jake, I'm happy to help. Someone will be there to show me what to do, right?"

"Sure, honey. All the other rallies I've attended ran like clockwork. I'm sure you can handle it, and it'll give you a chance to meet other EAA members. It might end up being a long day if the weather's good, but there's always someone around to give you a break."

"Well, that's reassuring," Chris replied.

"I'll introduce you to Ben Connor; he runs the ground crew. He'll be the one to assign you to your job and show you how it's done."

"Sounds like fun, and I'll get to see your plane in action. But you're still not getting me up in it."

Not a moment later, Frank Wilson walked into the diner hoping to find Jake, having already checked the airport. Jake, upon seeing his Army buddy, immediately stood. "Frank, how the hell are you?" Jake shouted above the noise.

Frank sat down at Jake's table. Seeing that someone was talking with Jake, Chris went over to the table. Both men stood as Chris put Jake's coffee mug down. "Frank, this is my girlfriend, Chris. Chris, Frank Wilson." Frank extended his hand and was surprised when Chris gave him a big hug. "Jake told me all about you and your beautiful niece. Thanks for not shooting him." The three laughed.

"What can I get you, Frank?"

"Just coffee today, Chris, thank you."

Jake read the expression on Frank's face. "You're

here to tell me that Kate's still having trouble in school, aren't you?"

"Yep, not social trouble, but from what my brother tells me she's still having a hard time with her schoolwork, and she hasn't touched the book you gave her."

"Maybe she's really not interested in flying, Frank. It's not an activity that you can talk someone into loving. They do or they don't. Some people were just born to fly."

"I agree, but I know how much she loved being in that plane, and she never stopped talking about it. I don't understand why she's having so much trouble, but I do know she loves flying."

"I'll tell you one thing," Jake said, taking a sip of coffee. "These kids today have it a lot tougher than we did growing up. There are so many things vying for their attention. I feel sorry for them."

"I don't have the answer," Frank admitted, "but I do know that Kate and her family are spending Thanksgiving with us. Kate has five days off, and her dad was hoping she might be able to get in the air again. You know, recharge her batteries or something."

Jake smiled as a thought came to mind. "Well, we're not going anywhere that day, or the following week. I might have an idea." With that, the two men began hatching a plan.

Chris glanced over and could see that something was brewing just from their body language.

Frank made a point of saying good-bye to Chris, stopping for a brief moment as he went up to pay his bill. "He's a good man," Frank sort of whispered.

"You both are," Chris replied with a smile. After Frank left, Chris grabbed Jake's order and took it to him.

"Kid not doing so hot?" she inquired.

"Ah, she's all right, just having a lot on her plate right now. Say, Chris, we don't have any plans for Thanksgiving, do we?"

Saturday morning dawned just as beautifully as the weatherman had predicted, and Clearview Airport was already buzzing with chapter members setting up for the big day. Jake was reinstalling the cowl of his Piper Cub when Chris drove up.

"Good morning, sweetheart," she said, after walking over to where Jake was working.

"Honey, give me a hand with this cowl. Hold on to the other side as I fasten these screws—after you give me a kiss, that is."

Chris gave Jake a quick peck on the lips, and crossed to the other side of the plane, holding the cowl as Jake fastened screws on the right side. "What's this all about?" she inquired.

"Just giving everything a once-over. I might end up giving a lot of rides today, depending on the crowd."

"I see you took some time to get all the bugs off," Chris observed, stepping aside to give Jake room to work on the left side.

"Yep, I want it to make a good impression."

"Well, I stopped off at the diner on the way over here and had the cook make us up two tins of scrambled eggs and home fries. Plus, I have coffee for the two of us. Why don't we sit at the table and have breakfast before the day gets started?"

"That's why I love you, baby, always looking after my stomach." Jake grabbed a rag to wipe his hands.

After breakfast, Chris walked to the office, impressed by how fast the chapter members were setting up. Two men were putting folding picnic tables on the grass in front of the office as others erected canopies for shade, while two other men staked out an area with caution tape, creating what Chris assumed would be a waiting area for children and parents. Closer to the office, women were busy setting up several grills and unloading supplies of hot dogs, buns, and drinks. Chris found the office and went in.

"Good morning, I'm Chris Fisher."

"Chris, pleased to meet you. Jake told me you were coming today. I'm Ben Connor. I'm so happy you volunteered to help out. Have you ever done anything like this before?"

"No, I haven't, Ben. I'm depending on you to fill me in."

Ben took his time going over the registration process with Chris, assuring her that another person would be along shortly to give her a hand.

Out on the flight line, airplanes were assembling to the right of the waiting area. Some of the pilots were looking over their aircraft and speaking with one another, waiting for the day's activities to begin. Jake taxied toward the office and made a hard right into the assembly area, lining up wingtip to wingtip with a four-seat Cessna 172. He climbed out of the Cub and stopped in to check on

Chris, and found her speaking with Linda Davis, the woman she would be working alongside.

Linda had three Young Eagles rallies under her belt and was an old hand at registering participants. Jake talked with the women for a minute, getting out of the way as the first families arrived. It didn't take long for the day to get going. "Jake, I've got one for you if you're ready," one of the helpers called out.

Jake walked over and greeted the family, shaking the young boy's hand. "Hello, young man. My name is Jake, and your name is...?"

The boy looked up with a big smile. "I'm Joseph Weber, sir. Are you a pilot?"

"I sure am, Joseph. Why don't all of us take a walk over to my airplane and I'll explain a few things to you and your parents before we go flying."

"My brother Ben will be here after his gymnastics lesson."

"Excellent. We have a great day to fly, Joseph, so let's get started."

And that's how it went throughout the day, families being ushered to and from airplanes, youngsters getting their first ride in a light aircraft, hot dogs, chips, and the opportunity for people to get a taste of general aviation at its finest. By noon, Jake was already on his fourth ride and was basically staying in the Cub as volunteers loaded and unloaded children, explaining the parts of the airplane as they went, while Jake signed their paperwork. Parents were given time to take pictures of their children in the cockpit wearing headphones before

Jake took off for another flight.

Inside the office, Chris and Linda stayed busy all day, helping families register, assigning flight numbers, and making sure loaders knew who was who. By the end of the day, the Napa Valley EAA chapter had given thirty-two flights.

Michelle Collins, the airport manager, had arranged for the local newspaper to do a story about the event and was happy when the photographer got some great shots of Jake's Cub. Michelle liked Jake and was pleased to see that he was finally dating, and happy to have a chance to talk with Chris for a while.

Registrations ended at 2:00, with the last rides finishing up by 3:00 that afternoon. Jake had just finished cleaning up the Cub by the time Chris made it back to the hangar.

"That was interesting," she said as she helped Jake push his plane back.

"Boy, we had a perfect day," he said, "nice and smooth for the kids, and the visibility was excellent."

"I know. This was a lot of fun; thank you for introducing me to these people. I couldn't get over how excited some of those kids were. One girl clapped as I tried handing her the application!" Chris laughed.

"I think I had her. She started clapping as we took off. I thought a tire was making noise," Jake admitted, shaking his head. "How about we go get some dinner."

"That's fine with me."

"Oh, one thing before I forget," Jake said before he pulled out. "I know you're cooking on Thanksgiving, but I might have something to do for an hour or so, and I'm not sure exactly what time I have to do it."

"You don't have to tell me what it's about, Jake. I've already figured that out for myself."

Chapter 13:
Thanksgiving

Kate opened her eyes to the sound of birds singing. The sophomore year had started off okay, but Kate felt as if she was already under water, and was happy to have a break. Yesterday's long ride from LA had done a number on her, and for a moment Kate didn't know where she was. But then she jumped out of bed and looked out the bedroom window at the tractor parked outside and it all came back.

She donned her robe and went downstairs. "Here's our sleepyhead," Frank announced as Kate made her entrance. Everyone in the kitchen clapped, making a mock big deal over her.

Kate grinned and curtsied, making everyone laugh. "Boy, that ride must have really knocked you out," Anna observed, walking over and giving her daughter a kiss. "Good morning, sweetheart."

"Good morning, everyone, sorry I overslept," Kate said, making the rounds.

"You don't have to apologize to us, Kate. I just got up, myself," Bob admitted as Kate hugged him.

"All right now, we're not having the big breakfast I usually make when you guys visit," Sue announced. "I put out oatmeal and fruit, so we'll all have a good appetite for turkey later on."

"That's fine with me," Kate replied.

"What time do you think we'll be eating, Sue?" Frank inquired.

"We'll be sitting down at around 2:00. Why, have a heavy date?"

"No, honey, I just wanted to know," Frank answered, giving Sue a wink. After breakfast, Frank went into his bedroom and dialed the phone. "We're all set for 1:00 p.m.," he said and hung up.

The morning went by quickly, between putting the turkey in the oven and watching the Macy's Thanksgiving Day Parade. Afterward, while the women were setting things up for the big feast, Frank came in from the porch. "Hey, Kate, why don't you get changed and take the tractor down to the lower vineyard. I planted the new vines you helped me with, and wanted to know what you thought about it."

Kate's face lit up. "Thanks, Uncle Frank. I was hoping I would get a chance to drive."

With that, Kate went off to get changed and out the door. Approaching the big tractor, Kate remembered the excitement of that first day, as the familiar smell of diesel and rubber carried her back to last summer. Then, with the turn of a key and push of a button, her old friend rumbled to life, the throaty sound of its engine serenading Kate down the road, and over the now-dried mud. Driving past the new vines her uncle had planted, Kate stopped and shut down. She heard the wind rustling the leaves as she reminisced about the first day she cut grass alone, and the sight of the small yellow plane high overhead.

"Wait!" Kate spun in her seat looking up, trying to

hear, turning her head. The airplane sound grew louder, echoing off the hills, until finally its direction became unmistakable. Kate turned just as a yellow airplane streaked over her head, right above the trees, and pulled up into a steep climb before banking to the left.

It was Jake!

The Cub's left wing dropped and the fuselage canted sideways, causing the small craft to seemingly drop out of the sky before straightening out and landing gently on the grass. Kate was amazed.

Jake climbed out as Kate hopped off the tractor and ran toward him, grinning.

"Hi, missy," Jake said.

"Jake, I'm so happy to see you! That was a beautiful landing."

"I'm happy to see you too, kiddo."

"Where's Chris, are you staying for Thanksgiving dinner?"

"Chris is cooking a turkey as we speak, so I can't stay long, I just wanted to drop in and see how you're doing with the book."

Kate looked down, realizing she had been set up. Jake saw the hurt in her eyes so explained, "Look, missy, I understand you're having a tough time at school. What's going on?"

Kate was angry and embarrassed. "Great! Now everyone knows how stupid I am. I'm sorry, I'm a slow reader."

"Heck, missy, that's nothing to be ashamed of. I was a lousy reader when I was a kid. In fact, I was so bad, I wrote book reports about movies I saw. But I got better at it, took a lot of work, but I did it. Listen, I know you can do this, and believe me, life is so much simpler when you're a good reader."

Kate just stood there, her eyes filling with tears. "I don't know what to do, Jake. I'm not lazy, I just feel stupid."

Jake squirmed; he'd not expected Kate to cry.

"Hold on, missy, I'm supposed to be cheering you up and giving you a pep talk!" He put his hands on his hips and shook his head. "Looks like I blew that one."

Kate started laughing through her tears. "This is a pep talk?"

Jake looked at her with a crooked smile and raised eyebrows. "Go team, go?"

Kate laughed harder, making Jake smile. "At least I made a good landing." The two looked at each other and hugged, then Jake gave Kate a pat on the back.

"Wipe those tears and walk me to the plane, kiddo. I have something for you."

Reaching the plane, Jake went into the bag strapped to the front seat and removed a long, thin, black book, opened it, and showed Kate the first few pages.

"Missy, this is a logbook. Every flight you make gets recorded right here. Date, aircraft type, registration number, flight times, destinations, everything. It's a legal record of your flight experience. I bought this for you after your first flight, and I've been logging all your hours ever since. You already have three hours logged."

Jake closed the book and handed it to her. "Look, I

know you can do this, kiddo, I didn't mean to make you upset. To make it up to you, how about we meet at the airport tomorrow and go flying."

Kate smiled as she inspected the entries Jake made. And tomorrow she was going to fly!

"Thank you, Jake!"

"Hey, maybe we can talk your parents into taking a short flight?"

Kate's smile got brighter. "My dad will love it, but good luck with my mom."

"Let's just see what happens. Now drive that thing back up to the house and have a wonderful meal, and tell your uncle to give me a call so we can set things up."

Kate stopped for a moment. "He set this whole thing up, didn't he?"

"He loves you, missy, and he worries about you, and he figured seeing me might put some wind back in your sails." Jake gave Kate a hug and walked back to the Cub.

Kate drove the tractor slowly back toward the house after watching Jake take off.

As Kate shut down, the excitement of Jake's visit and an upcoming flight was replaced by dismay over the revelation that everyone knew about her troubles in school. Her emotions bounced from one extreme to the other—excitement, determination, resignation, disappointment—all had their turn. When Kate entered the kitchen, her expression gave her away.

"Katie, what's wrong?" Anna said. Sue spun around from the sink, Frank and Bob looked at each other and turned off the TV.

Kate looked at her mom and the words just spilled out. "Jake landed in the field next to the vines, Uncle Frank had told him about my schoolwork and he came to give me a pep talk. Everyone knows how stupid I am."

Kate stood motionless for a moment, mortified that her emotions had gotten the best of her. Then she turned and ran up to her room, her mother close behind.

Sue looked at Frank. "So that's why you winked at me!"

Bob attempted to come to his brother's defense. "Frank, that was a great idea, I think..."

Sue shot him a look that said, *I'll deal with you two knuckleheads later*, then commanded in a stern tone, "Frank, carve the turkey, I'm going upstairs."

Anna and Sue reappeared a few minutes later and put the food on the table as Frank finished carving the turkey.

"Is she all right?"

Anna looked at her brother-in-law with a kind smile. "She's fine, Frank, and she's not mad at you at all. She's getting changed and will be down in a minute. She was happy to see Jake again, and he gave her something that she's excited to show all of you. And, after dinner, she agreed that we're all going to have a talk."

Kate came down in time to help her aunt and mother, then thrilled everyone with a vivid description of Jake's arrival before explaining the logbook as everyone enjoyed the Thanksgiving feast.

After dinner, the family retired to the living room,

Kate sitting next to her mother. Sue passed a tray of after-dinner mints around, starting things off as she reached her niece. "Okay, Kate, tell us what's going on at school that has you stumped."

Kate paused a moment, handed the mints to her mom, and looked up. "I read slow, Aunt Sue; my homework takes me forever."

"Well," Frank jumped in, "that's the first step in problem-solving, knowing that you have a problem."

Sue sat across from her and continued, "I don't know that you read all that slow, honey. You had some trouble with the recipe you helped me with during the summer, but you did get it after a bit."

"I think it has to do with me. I just...I have a hard time understanding what I'm reading," Kate confessed.

"Second step," Frank coached, "identify the problem."

"We can get a reading tutor as soon as we get back home," Anna offered, looking to her husband for approval.

"Fine with me," Bob added.

"That's a great suggestion, Anna, and it's the third step in problem-solving: coming up with solutions. A tutor is a great one."

"Here's another suggestion, and it has to do with something that's obvious, and yet invisible," Bob announced, standing up and walking over to where his daughter sat. Everyone watched, not knowing what Bob was getting at, until he reached down and took Kate's cell phone from her hand.

Bob held the small device above his head and

swung it high in front of the family, speaking as a lawyer would to a jury. "I'd like to present for everyone's consideration what I feel is the main cause of Kate's problem. We'll call it Exhibit A, the cell phone. Never in history has there been a device more distracting than this little thing. For the life of me, I can't figure out how anything gets done anymore. People are so consumed by the ability to instantly interact with each other that they never concentrate on the task at hand. It's almost as if living is nothing more than a bother, getting in the way of their texting."

He pivoted to stand in front of his daughter. "Kate, this is your biggest challenge right here—figuring out what place this thing has in your life, and realizing that a lot of your stress is caused by trying to do too many things at the same time. There! I said my piece."

Bob handed the phone back to his daughter and sat down. Sue, wanting to keep Kate from becoming defensive, stood up. "Well, Kate, how about helping me put dessert out before everyone falls asleep."

Kate didn't say anything and followed her aunt. Once in the kitchen, Sue turned and gave her niece a big hug.

"Don't be too hard on yourself, sweetheart. You're a very smart young woman. I'm sure you'll come up with a way to keep your parents and your friends happy. Now help me put these pies on the table and I'll get the coffee."

Nothing more was said about Kate's dilemma during dessert, or the impromptu game of charades that ensued afterward. It was just past 11:00 when Kate told

136

everyone she was turning in for the night. "Mom, the tutor is a great idea, and Dad, I promise I will take everything you said to heart and do something about it. It will take a few weeks, but I promise things will improve."

"We know you'll figure something out, dear. Sleep tight," her mother said.

Kate went up to her room, knowing that she had to act but putting off starting until after a long sleep.

# # #

The cool morning air through the open window ruffled Kate's hair as she rode in the back seat of her father's car. She went over in her head everything that Jake had taught her that summer. Arriving at the airport, the Wilsons walked around to the front of the office to wait for Jake.

"There he is!" Kate pointed to the small yellow dot in the sky, accompanied by the faint drone of an engine. She looked at her dad, excited that he agreed to take the first ride. All watched as the Cub made a perfect landing and came to a stop on the apron. A short time later, Bob, strapped into the front seat, smiled like a kid in a candy store as Jake taxied to the runway, lined up, and took to the sky.

After the flight, Bob just kept shaking his head, saying, "Wow, beautiful, just beautiful!" Jake also gave a ride to Sue, who had never ridden in a small plane. Of course, she also was smiling as she climbed out. "That was fantastic!" was all she could speak.

After thanking Jake, Sue ran over and gave her husband a big kiss for talking her into going, then looked at

Kate. "Now I see what all the fuss is about. What a great view!"

Kate just smiled. Anna gave her daughter a big hug and told her to be careful before Kate climbed into the front seat of the Cub and put on her headset before buckling up.

Kate was all business as she held the brakes while Jake gave the prop a spin, bringing the engine back to life.

"Okay, missy, it's all yours," Jake said after fastening his belts. "Let's see if you remember anything I taught you."

Kate inched the throttle forward, listening to the engine pick up speed as she swung the plane's nose to the left and right.

Kate used the heel brakes at the hold line, performed her final check, looked for traffic, and moved the Cub onto the runway for takeoff. But instead of taking off, she again sat for just a moment, looking down the runway through the spinning propeller, listening to the soft steady hum of the engine. *God, I want this*, she thought just before the spell was broken by the man in the back seat.

"Everything okay up there?"

"Yep, I was just savoring the moment," Kate again answered as she advanced the throttle. Jake smiled, staying on the controls. Not since August had Kate felt such exhilaration as she guided the plane down the runway, doing her best to stay right over the center line. She eased the craft into the sky, again feeling the magic as she broke ground to swim in the ocean of air.

138

Once airborne, Jake reminded Kate to keep her head on a swivel and scan for traffic.

"Let's level off at three thousand feet."

"Why are we going so high, Jake?"

"Let's head out to the east a few miles and I'll show you," Jake replied as he scanned for traffic.

Kate continued her climb, making small course changes every minute, which allowed her to look for traffic ahead of the climbing plane.

"Great work, missy, I like the way you clear the air ahead of us."

"Thanks, Jake. I wasn't sure if you'd notice."

"I notice everything, kiddo, keep up the good work. Now, when we level off, I'm going to demonstrate how to perform a forward slip. By slipping you can increase your rate of descent without gaining speed. You saw how I shoehorned the plane into that small field on Thursday."

"I was wondering how you did that," Kate said, looking over her shoulder.

She leveled off at the assigned altitude, reduced power, and waited to feel the familiar wag of the stick telling her that Jake had the controls.

"Okay, missy," Jake said as he took over with the expected stick shake. "I've got it. Kate, you already know that banking left will cause the nose of the plane to yaw right, if we don't use the rudder to counteract adverse yaw. Well, in a forward slip we're going to bank left and use the rudder to hold the nose further to the right. That's going to present the left side of the fuselage to the oncoming air, increasing drag. It's a maneuver you have to master in order to get the most out of this old bird. Okay, here we go."

Jake applied a bit of carb heat and reduced power to idle, then lowered the left wing and used the rudder to swing the nose to the right.

"We control airspeed by lowering or raising the nose, but don't get too slow or she'll spin." The plane descended with the nose pointed fifteen degrees to the right. The little plane shook a bit and the wind noise increased as Kate looked out the left to see where they were going.

"Look at the altimeter unwind, Kate; we have a healthy rate of descent and we're still holding sixty miles an hour. Now I'm going to seamlessly ease off the rudder, and raise the low wing."

"Wow, that's amazing, Jake."

"Okay, now it's your turn. Let's fly straight and level for a few minutes. I want you to think about lowering the left wing and adding right rudder at the same time. I want the plane headed in the same direction it is now as you go in and out of the slip."

"Okay, I'll give it a try," Kate said, visualizing the inputs.

"Any time you're ready, go ahead."

Kate did her best, but between adding too much rudder or not enough aileron to hold the wing down, she was all over the sky. After several tries, Kate began to get the hang of it, giving the plane smooth flight control inputs. Jake had her hold the slip in and play with varying degrees of input until she could hold the plane on course with a full slip.

"Wow, I'm exhausted!" Kate remarked after the workout.

Jake laughed. "Good. Now let's practice a right forward slip."

"No, I need to rest for a minute," Kate pleaded.

"No rush, kiddo."

Kate rested a moment, then lowered the right wing, kicking in the left rudder. Again the plane seemed to have a mind of its own.

"This is harder than the left slip, Jake. I'm all over the place."

"Funny how that works." Jake laughed. "Don't worry, everyone has trouble going the opposite way the first few times. Come on now, just think about it, then do it."

On the ground, Bob watched intently as the small yellow plane wobbled around like a drunken sailor. "I don't know what they're doing, but it sure doesn't look like a plain-old joy ride to me."

Frank just kept watching until the small craft finally approached the airport. "They seem to be getting ready to land, let's see how she does," he said as he walked onto the taxiway to watch.

"All right, Kate, I want you to hold pattern altitude until I tell you to turn base."

Kate realized what was coming next, hoping Jake didn't ask for a right slip. "Okay, Kate, carb heat, engine to idle, and turn base."

Kate's anxiety grew as she saw how high she was turning final.

"Now concentrate on airspeed and give me a left slip, heading straight for the grass."

"They're high," Frank announced, watching what he expected to be an overshoot. To his amazement, the yellow plane started to fly cockeyed toward the runway, dropping like a stone from its lofty height until it was one hundred feet or so above the grass, then gracefully straightened out, executing a smooth landing just past the numbers.

"What do you call that?" Bob said to no one in particular. Anna just watched, not saying a word.

They could already see the smile on their daughter's face as the Cub turned off the taxiway and pulled in between the two hangars.

"Look how happy she is," Anna remarked, as she smiled and waved.

Kate yelled from the cockpit, "Did you see that, Dad? That was me! Remember what I told you yesterday about the slip? Well, I just used it!"

Jake just smiled as he came around and joined everyone by the hangar.

"Well, she got a good workout, didn't you, kiddo?"

"I know, Mom, I worked so hard to learn that maneuver, I feel like I just ran a marathon." Everyone laughed.

"She did real good, folks. Kate's very comfortable in the air, she has a natural ability, she's eager to learn, and she picks up everything I teach her right away." Jake turned to Kate for emphasis. "And she promised me that she is making changes at home. Right, missy?"

"Jake, I'm not going to let you, or anyone else, down—I know what I have to do."

"You'll have plenty of help, the way I see it, so how about helping me put this bird away so you can get out of here," Jake said with a smile. "Your mom told me you're off to visit a friend."

Kate blushed and gave her mother a look. "Mom!"

After cleaning up, Jake spun around in his chair, looked at his Cub, and smiled. It was a good day.

Bruce and Kate sat together on the back porch of his family's home, admiring the rows of grapevines as the setting sun created the perfect autumn panorama. Sue had arranged the visit to make sure Kate and Bruce got to spend some time together, and so Anna could meet Bruce's mom.

Kate and Bruce talked a while, then just sat quietly until Kate said, "You're right, Bruce, it is peaceful here. I love the openness; it reminds me of where we lived before moving to LA."

"I've never lived anywhere else," Bruce admitted. "So to me this is normal. I like the city, and I like all the things there are to do in cities. But this is where I belong."

Kate started to reach over to hold Bruce's hand, but her mom, aunt, and Bruce's mom came out onto the porch, ready to go, right on cue.

###

Back at School, Kate put her new strategy into action. At lunch she made it known to her friends that after school she would be away from her phone until later on in the evening. The funny thing was that no one seemed put off by her announcement, and Jess commented that she also was going to have to cool texting until after dinner, so she could knock out the writing assignment she had.

That week, Kate finally mentioned her flying activities and what Jake had told her about the EAA to her science teacher, Mr. Rice. During the conversation, Mr. Rice admitted that he hadn't flown in over seven years, but after seeing how invested his pupil was, he began investigating the EAA and all it had to offer, and decided to bring the science of aviation into his classroom.

Mr. Rice was pleasantly surprised to find that many of his students had an interest in aviation, which encouraged him to investigate a program he had read about online. Getting a go-ahead from the school's administration took several weeks of hard work and persistence, but finally Mr. Rice received permission to present his idea to his students. A week later, as the students entered the classroom, it became apparent that Mr. Rice had a guest speaker.

"All right, class. As you all know, Kate Wilson became interested in aviation over the past summer and is now taking flying lessons. In case some of you don't know, I earned my pilot's license almost ten years ago. Since our conversation, I started researching the group Kate mentioned, called the EAA. It was formed in the early

1950s by pilots who were building their own airplanes, so they could share information about construction techniques, new innovations, and safety. Since that time, the EAA has grown tremendously with local chapters worldwide. I've invited the president of the very first EAA chapter, located not far from here, to tell you about a special program that some of you might be interested in. Class, may I introduce Mr. Bob McDonnell."

All eyes turned to the gray-haired man as he walked over to Mr. Rice, shook the teacher's hand, and introduced himself. Over the next twenty minutes, Mr. McDonnell spoke about the impact general aviation made on the local economy, career opportunities in the aviation field, and the Young Eagles program. "Now, for the best part, there is a program not affiliated with the EAA called Build-A-Plane. It brings together donated planes in need of restoration, or partially completed kit planes, and schools, providing an opportunity for students to learn about aircraft construction as they work on a project. Your teacher will be taking names of students who might be interested in participating in a build project. If Mr. Rice finds enough student interest, and if all goes well, your school will apply for a project. EAA members will provide mentoring, but fund-raising and work on the plane will be done by you students. Although it might take time to find a project, it didn't stop your teacher from already getting permission from the school administration and securing a space in the automotive shop. He even talked about fund-raising ideas with members of the Parent-Teacher Organization."

Hands shot up when Mr. McDonnell asked for questions. Kate, however, just sat there not believing what she was hearing. She had a huge smile on her face as she changed classes.

"Jess, I'm so glad you told me about Mr. Rice. I can't believe we might get a plane to build!"

Jess smiled. "Yeah, I didn't see that coming."

Both girls laughed. As soon as she got home, Kate called her uncle and told him the news, and asked him to pass it along to Jake.

Chapter 14:
Mrs. Plum

Anna closed her book after hearing the doorbell, and answered the door to find a thin, gray-haired woman patiently waiting. "Hello, I'm Mrs. Plum."

"Please come in, Mrs. Plum! I'm Anna Wilson, it's so nice to meet you."

The slight woman, who had spent forty years in the classroom, picked up her bag and entered the apartment as Kate emerged from her room.

"We are so happy that you agreed to tutor our daughter," Anna said as she showed the teacher into the kitchen.

Mrs. Plum, not wanting to sit at home after retirement, had started tutoring students as a way of getting out of the house. Now in her tenth year, she couldn't imagine not tutoring and loved helping students realize their potential one-on-one. What had convinced Kate's mother to call Mrs. Plum was the fact that she made house calls.

"Mrs. Plum, this is my daughter, Kate."

"Hello, Kate, it's a pleasure to meet you."

"Thank you for doing this, Mrs. Plum," Kate said, shaking the tutor's hand.

"Will the kitchen be all right to work in?" Anna queried, "and can I get you anything, water, perhaps?"

"That will be very fine, dear, thank you."

Mrs. Plum took a seat at the table and motioned for her new student to sit next to her. Kate complied then, as instructed, opened the book Mrs. Plum handed her. "All right, dear, let's get started. Please start reading aloud from chapter one. But before you do, I want you to remember this." Mrs. Plum paused. "There has never been a case of someone working hard and not overcoming a reading disability. Yes, it is hard work, but soon you will find that your ability to read will seem as natural as speaking, your speed will increase, and you will understand and enjoy everything you read. Now begin."

Anna hovered for a moment before retreating to the living room, pretending to read as she listened in on the lesson.

The teacher sat quietly, observing and listening as Kate read, then asked her to explain the chapter. Kate felt nervous, and hesitated, struggling to remember.

"All right, dear, let's stop for a moment."

Mrs. Plum leaned into Kate, looking around first as if to make sure no one else could hear her.

"Now listen closely, dear," she said, almost in a whisper. "I'm going to tell you the secret to better reading."

She slammed her hand on the table and shouted, "PAY ATTENTION, PAY ATTENTION, PAY ATTENTION!" her left hand pounding the table with each word.

Anna jumped up startled by the outburst wondering what had just happened.

Shocked, Kate sat with her mouth open.

"Now," Mrs. Plum asked in a pleasant tone, "How

do we read better, Kate?"

"Pay attention?" Kate answered meekly.

"Progress!" the old woman shouted, raising her right index finger above her head for effect. "Funny how everyone gets that one right."

Anna, shocked but smiling, shook her head, and sat back on the couch to continue her reading.

Mrs. Plum explained her point. "Kate, a lot of people read the same way they watch television; they are inattentive and passive. Understanding what you read takes effort, and you must make the effort." Again, she asked Kate to read aloud, but this time it was like a light had been turned on in Kate's head. She found it hard to pay attention to what she read but she did, able to give Mrs. Plum a summary after each chapter. "Progress," the tutor again announced when the lesson ended.

And so it went, every week a new lesson, and a new assignment. At first, Kate thought her tutor was a little crazy, but as time went by, she grew to enjoy their weekly visit. What Kate loved most about Mrs. Plum was her introduction to every session. "There has never been a case of someone working hard and not overcoming a reading disability. Now let us begin."

Mrs. Plum was patient and demanding at the same time. She understood the frustration slow readers face, while never tolerating self-pity or laziness. Kate was not lazy, nor felt sorry for herself. Besides, Mrs. Plum would have none of it. "No pity parties allowed," she would declare in a loud voice, her finger held above her head.

Kate learned to read in a questioning manner as if

searching for something. It helped when she took the heading of a chapter and turned it into a question; for example, changing "The Causes of the Civil War" into the question, "What were the causes of the Civil War?"

That gave her something to look for, something to find out. Kate no longer moved her lips, learning that she could read faster than she could talk, and learned not to reread the same phrase over and over, as it was better to pay closer attention the first time. Mrs. Plum had Kate use her right hand to guide her eyes along the passage, which helped focus her attention on what she was reading. Over time, Kate learned to move her hand faster and faster, finding that she was no longer reading every word individually. Her mind could process what she was reading in complete sentences. Soon Kate didn't need her fingers to guide the way. After a lot of practice, the results of her hard work began to show. Kate's grades improved, and with that, her confidence. Not only was she reading faster, she now had the time to read her flying manual, *Stick and Rudder*, and understand it.

Several weeks later, Kate pushed back from her desk after finishing a writing assignment and reflected on how much she had accomplished. She felt such warmth and gratitude for the woman who had lifted her spirits and furnished her with the tools she needed to excel. It was all coming together!

Chapter 15:
The RANS S-7

In the second week of February, Kate and Jess had just stepped off the school bus on their way into school when Kate noticed a man that she recognized standing next to a truck with a large wooden crate sitting on its flatbed.

"Jess, I think that's Mr. McDonnell. He's the man that's trying to get an airplane for the school."

"Well, it looks like Mr. Rice is in for quite a surprise," Jess said, smiling as she held the door for her friend. Their homeroom was located on the other side of the building, which did not afford them a view of the road, but the news spread through the school like wildfire, so Kate had already heard the news in the hall before entering Mr. Rice's classroom for her third-period science class.

Mr. Rice and Mr. McDonnell were standing in front of the room, both of them smiling. "Okay, class, settle down; we have a big announcement to make," Mr. Rice began. "As you remember, Mr. McDonnell from EAA Chapter 1, working together with the Build-A-Plane Program, was trying to find an aircraft project for our school. To explain to you further what's been going on, I'll turn the floor over once again to Mr. McDonnell."

Bob McDonnell stepped forward. "I'm sure most of you got a good look at the flatbed truck with the wooden crate on it as you arrived at school this morning. I'm happy to announce that inside that crate is a RANS S-7 Courier airplane kit. The kit was donated to the Build-A-Plane Program by the estate of a deceased EAA member in Arizona. I and several members drove out over the weekend and transported it back here, and I'm sure they are unloading it as we speak."

Everyone started clapping and talking, and it took a few minutes for the class to settle down after the announcement, allowing Mr. McDonnell to hand out pictures of a completed RANS S-7.

"Mr. Rice will be in charge of setting up after-school and weekend work schedules and will notify me once the crate has been unloaded, and a full inventory of parts completed. I'm looking forward to working with you students, and we have three other chapter members who have volunteered to help ensure the successful completion of this project. Now, the one thing the project did not come with is an engine. I'll continue to search for a suitable engine for your project. In the meantime, I understand the Parent Teacher Organization is going to set up fund-raising events to help things along."

The rest of the day flew by as if there was a buzz in the school. Everyone was talking about the crate that had gone into the shop that contained an airplane.

# # #

The first Saturday in March brought cloudy skies and showers and was the first weekend Kate was able to work on the new school project. In all, fifteen students had volunteered to help build the airplane, and over the last few weeks, together with Mr. Rice and Mr. McDonnell, they had finished inventory and setting up.

The RANS S-7 Courier was a two-place, high-wing taildragger much like Jake's Piper Cub, and was referred to as a rag-and-tube aircraft. The fuselage and tail were made of Chromoly steel tubes welded together to form a very light and strong structure. Dacron fabric would serve as the skin of the aircraft, wrapping around and overlapping the tubes, with a strong glue holding it in place. The wings were aluminum tubes, gussets, and plastic fuel tanks that would all be covered over by fabric, which would act as the skin of the wing. As the day began, Kate and two other girls were given the job of building wing ribs. The girls gathered all of the parts, tubes, and rivets called out in the directions. Kate, Cheryl, and Michelle took turns placing the pre-bent tubes and gussets in slots cut into a plywood jig, which held everything in place, then drilled holes for the rivets. The girls learned that after all of the holes were drilled, parts had to be removed from the jig, to deburr the holes, before being placed back into the jig and riveted together. In all, twenty-two ribs had to be fabricated, eleven for each wing.

While that was going on, other students were pre-fitting floor panels and rudder pedals, while still others assembled ailerons and flaps. All under the watchful eye of the EAA mentors. The shop was a beehive of activity that day, with Mr. Rice, beaming as he walked around with his camera, taking pictures of students working on this and that. The parents in attendance set up coffee and doughnuts in the morning and treated everyone to pizza that afternoon.

The pace was slow and deliberate, with an emphasis on safety and quality.

First, chapter members explained what had to be done, what tools were needed, and the precautions that had to be taken to accomplish the task safely. The importance of quality was demonstrated after Cheryl called one of the EAA mentors over. "Excuse me, sir, this wing gusset looks like it might have been bent, or stepped on. It looks like it was bent back into shape. Is that okay?"

The EAA mentor studied the part for a moment. "You have a good eye, Cheryl. This was a great catch. No, we're not going to use it. I'll show this to Bob and have him order a replacement. Great job, girls!"

After showing the damaged part to the other students, they all were reminded that mistakes happen, and were no big deal. It was easy to order new parts, as only the best went into the finished product.

That evening Kate called Bruce, smiling to herself.

"Hi, Kate, how are things in LA?"

"Well, the San Andreas Fault opened up and LA is slipping into the sea."

Bruce laughed. "You doofus, it slipped into the sea last time you called me!"

Both laughed even harder. Kate and Bruce talked for almost an hour about everything, finally ending their conversation with the customary, "It was nice talking to you."

After the call, Kate sat at her desk, wondering when she would get the nerve to tell Bruce how much she missed him.

By early April, the RANS wings had been constructed and the fuselage had everything pre-fitted and then removed to facilitate covering. Kate attended a class on covering given by the members of Chapter 1. The process, demonstrated in a training video, had to be strictly adhered to. Basically the Dacron fabric was draped over and glued to the frame. Covering went well, with all students getting a chance to cover different parts of the plane—flaps, ailerons, and elevators first, then the wings. The students, using a household iron set at two hundred fifty degrees, shrank the fabric in place, with each student shrinking a portion of the skin. Then the iron was set at three hundred fifty degrees and the fabric ironed again, shrinking it as tight as a drum to the structure.

Covering went slowly, but by the end of the school year, only the fuselage had yet to be covered. Now the wings looked more like an airplane, and less like a jungle gym.

When June arrived, Kate took stock of her sophomore year. She had improved her grades and managed to stay connected with friends, even though she never looked at her phone between the hours of 5:00 and 8:00 p.m. She had read *Stick and Rudder*, stayed in touch with Bruce, and was looking forward to seeing him in a few weeks. She and Jess were tighter than ever, and Jess's mom was to be married to a very nice man. Their school was building an airplane, of all things, and with the end of the school year just weeks away, Kate would be back in the sky.

Oh, and one more thing that made up this good year. Thanks to Mrs. Plum, Kate was living proof that there had never been a case of someone working hard and not overcoming a reading disability.

Chapter 16:
The Mighty 150

Sitting in the left seat of a different airplane, brakes set, right hand on the throttle and left hand on the ignition key, a very apprehensive Kate looked left and right. Yes, her trusted instructor was with her, but he was sitting next to, not behind, her, and just before she yelled "Clear!" and started the engine, that friend and instructor said, "Stop."

So much had happened in the week before this unsettling moment—the school year ended, she had said good-bye to friends, and again wiped tears from her eyes as her father drove back to Los Angeles. Kate was happy that her mother had decided to spend July with her at the vineyard.

All of this was expected, as were the butterflies in her stomach as she waited for Bruce the night he took her to a movie. What she didn't expect was to be in a different aircraft, yet here she sat, in a Cessna 150, the venerable workhorse of the training fleet. It was Kate's first meeting with Jake since Thanksgiving, and Jake had met her in the parking lot instead of the hangar and walked her out to the apron in front of the office, telling her he wanted to show her something. There sat the old high-wing, tricycle-gear airplane with an orange and white paint scheme.

"What type of plane is this?" Kate had asked.

"It's a Cessna 150, the airplane you're going to take lessons in, missy."

"I thought I would be flying in the Cub," Kate said in a disappointed tone.

"Sorry, Kate, you're going to have to learn a whole lot more than just stick and rudder skills to become a pilot. This aircraft is equipped with radio navigation, and an attitude indicator, something the Cub doesn't have. And as you can see, it has a nose wheel, so landing and taxiing will be different."

Jake and Kate untied the wings and walked around the airplane as Jake explained the preflight inspection. As he talked, Kate felt overwhelmed as she climbed into the left-hand seat and buckled in. Jake explained the engine start procedure and waited to see if Kate would proceed. Kate put her hand on the throttle and reached for the key, not sure why this feeling of uncertainty was making it so hard to think. Then Jake put his hand over her right hand.

"Stop."

"What?" Kate looked at Jake.

"Stop," he again said. "How do you feel right now?"

"I have a bad feeling I'm not ready for this. I feel confused—you went too fast."

"All right, Kate, take a deep breath." Jake unbuckled his seat belt. "Get out and tie it back down, then meet me in the hangar." With that, Jake got out and walked away.

Kate just sat there bewildered, then gathered

herself, put the plane away and walked into the hangar.

"Have a seat, Kate," Jake said. On the table was a book, the Cessna Model 150 owner's manual.

"I'm sorry, kiddo, but trying to explain that uneasy feeling never leaves the same impression as actually living it."

"I know, I still feel upset," Kate admitted, sitting next to her instructor.

"I understand, and I want you to never forget that feeling in your gut. It's going to keep you out of trouble. This business of flying is unforgiving of the careless and unprepared. I purposely created a situation where an authoritative figure was pushing you to do something that you weren't prepared for or disagreed with. Remember, you always have the right to question authority!"

"So I should have said no, I don't want to fly?" Kate questioned.

"You could, or you could just confess that you didn't feel ready to fly, without full knowledge of the new aircraft and its systems. No professional is ever going to argue with that, and if they do, you don't want to fly with them, anyway."

Kate looked down at the floor and shook her head. "Boy, did I feel uneasy."

"Hard lessons are not easily forgotten. Now shake it off, and let's get started on today's lesson: the aircraft pilot's operating handbook, or POH."

Kate settled in to listen. Jake explained, "Before flying a different type of airplane, pilots are required to study the POH. It contains operating limitations, instrument markings, and information the manufacturer considers pertinent for the safe operation of the aircraft. And you will be expected to take flight training and a check ride before being signed off in your logbook that you are qualified to fly that model plane."

Thus Kate attended her first hour of ground school. The lesson began with the flight and ground school curriculum necessary for Kate to earn her pilot's license. Then Jake guided Kate through the Cessna 150 POH.

At noon, Jake suggested that the two go to the diner for lunch.

"That's a great idea, Jake, I could use a break," Kate admitted.

Chris greeted teacher and student as the pair walked into the diner.

"Hi, sweetheart, how are you?" Chris asked as she gave Kate a big hug. "That old crank wasn't too hard on you, was he?"

Jake just shook his head. "Take it easy on me, Chris. You know it's hard enough teaching these kids anything today, and to make matters worse, this one's a girl!"

Kate spun around at the remark as Chris shot back, "Hey, watch it there, Jake, or this girl won't bring you anything to eat."

Kate just shook her head and laughed. Chris took her break and joined Kate and Jake for lunch, making sure Kate got a nice big piece of cake for dessert. After lunch, Jake asked Kate if she wanted to take another look at the 150, adding that if she felt comfortable enough, they would fly.

This time Kate was a pro, performing a thorough preflight, using the Preflight Checklist as she went along, before climbing in and buckling up.

Strapped into the right seat, Jake asked Kate for the checklist. "Okay, Kate, before we start, what runway are you planning to use, and in what direction are we departing the traffic pattern?"

Kate was quick with the answer. "Winds are out of the north, so I plan to use runway one. We'll depart the pattern straight out to the north, before turning east to the practice area."

"Excellent. I agree. Now we can begin. I'll read the checklist item by item; your job will be to perform each task, and confirm that you did it. All right, let's get started."

After running through the Before Starting Engine Checklist, Jake took a moment. "All set there, missy?"

Kate's heart began to beat faster as excitement in her grew, for she was preparing to fly a new, and more complex, airplane.

"All set."

Jake started from the top.

"Altimeter set, remember ninety feet."

Kate spun the knob on the altimeter until it indicated the field elevation. "Check."

"Mixture—full rich; remember, that means all the way in."

Kate pushed the mixture knob all the way in. "Check."

"Carburetor heat—cold."

Kate checked the square carburetor heat handle, making sure it was all the way in. "Check."

"Brakes—set and hold."

Kate pushed on the top of each rudder pedal. "Check," she replied through her smile.

"Master switch—on."

"Check."

Kate and Jake took a moment to don their headsets before continuing.

"Prime as required." Kate gave the primer knob two pumps and locked it. "Check."

"Throttle—open a quarter inch."

Kate set the throttle. "Check."

"Propeller area clear."

Kate looked around, no one in sight, and yelled out the window. "Clear!"

"Ignition switch—start."

Kate, filled with anticipation, smiled, took another quick look around, and turned the key. Around and around the propeller blades spun, as the Mighty 150 coughed a moment and sprang to life, shaking the airframe as it strained against the brakes.

Now in a louder voice against the noise of the engine, Jake continued, "Throttle—one thousand rpm, and check for oil pressure."

Kate pulled the throttle back a bit, watching the tachometer. "Check!" she answered after making sure the oil pressure gauge read in the green.

"Radio on and set to one two two point eight."

"Check."

"Transponder to stand by, and set to twelve hundred."

"Check."

"All right, Kate, back off the throttle, roll forward and check the brakes, then let's turn toward the taxiway nice and easy."

The 150 had a yoke instead of a stick, sort of a sawed-off steering wheel that she could turn side to side, and pull in and out. The rudder pedals were still used to taxi but now controlled the nose gear as well as the rudder.

"Very good, Kate. Now taxi down to the hold line, keeping the nose over the center line."

Kate kept glancing at the instrument panel festooned with round dials, radios, and an artificial horizon.

To her, the 150 felt like a brand-new and very modern airplane, when in fact it had been built in 1967. With production starting in 1958, and over twenty-three thousand built, the Cessna 150 was the most widely used trainer in the world, with thousands still in use. Large flaps that could extend to forty degrees, a hundred-horsepower engine that allowed for short takeoff performance, and stout landing gear made the Cessna 150 an excellent training platform.

Once at the hold line, Jake read item by item from the Before Takeoff Checklist.

"Cabin doors—latched."

"Check."

"Flight controls—free, and correct."

162

Kate pulled the yoke in and out and turned it side to side. "Check."

"Elevator trim—takeoff position."

"Check."

"Transponder to ALT."

Kate felt like an airline pilot as she reached for the device that would send signals to Air Traffic Control—ATC—radar, turning its small knob from standby to altitude. "Check."

Kate was aware of everything around her, the powerful engine, the prop blast shaking the plane, and all the dials on the panel in front of her. She was so excited!

Jake talked Kate through the run-up procedure, advancing the throttle and checking each magneto, then continued.

"Kate, airports without control towers are assigned radio frequencies, allowing aircraft arriving and departing to broadcast their intentions and position. We use this common traffic advisory frequency, or CTAF, to coordinate our movements with other aircraft. You have the radio set to 122.8, which is the frequency assigned to this airport. I'm going to broadcast the airport name, who we are, what we are doing, and again the airport name, in case a pilot didn't hear the beginning of our call."

Kate listened, intent on understanding Jake's call.

"Clearview traffic, Cessna two two seven three, departing runway one, departing to the north, Clearview."

He waited a moment then said, "All right, missy, no one has responded, so let's make sure no one is on final. Remember, winds are straight down the runway, so ailerons neutral."

Kate took a long look downwind. "The pattern looks clear."

"Okay, Kate, it's all yours."

Kate tingled with excitement. She was making the decision: go or no go!

Again checking for traffic, Kate advanced the throttle and released the brakes, steering the Cessna onto the center line of the runway, then smoothly adding all the power the trainer had. As they accelerated, Kate kept glancing at her airspeed and oil pressure, making sure everything was good to go.

Feeling the controls come alive, Kate began increasing back pressure as Jake coached her through her first takeoff in the new bird. She was immediately aware of how much heavier the Cessna felt than the Cub.

When the plane left the ground, Kate instinctively added a bit of right rudder as it began to climb, quickly adapting her control inputs to adjust to the slower control response of the trainer.

"Good job, kiddo. Now let's hold this runway heading to one thousand feet, then turn to ninety degrees, and climb to three thousand as we head east toward the practice area."

During the hour-and-a-half flight, Jake had Kate stall the aircraft, and perform slow flight and shallow turns. Kate also simulated a landing pattern, while still at altitude, slowing the aircraft down and adding flaps in increments to see how the new plane handled. She listened to the whirr of the electric motor as the flaps came down, thrilled that she was flying a plane more complex than the Cub. The toughest part of the lesson was learning how to abort a landing by going around.

Jake talked Kate through the procedure, as adding full power with flaps deployed and nose-up trim might result in the plane ballooning, and getting dangerously slow. Kate performed the procedure several times, alarmed at first by the force needed to hold the nose down until the trim was adjusted, but kept at it until she became proficient.

"I'm surprised how much faster the Cessna loses altitude after deploying full flaps. You don't have to slip to lose altitude in this plane," Kate remarked.

"Most modern aircraft have flaps just for that reason, Kate. They allow for a steep, stabilized approach, and slower landing speeds. Now let's head back to the airport and give it a try. This time I'll coach you through the radio calls."

"Okay, Jake, I'm looking forward to it."

Kate got a chance to relax somewhat as the Mighty 150 flew west. She loved looking at the Earth from above, and never took for granted how lucky she was to have walked over to that open hangar door almost a year ago. But now it was time to get back to work.

Kate went over in her head what she would say on the radio, at each phase of the pattern, and thought through the steps she needed to accomplish to land.

"Clearview traffic, Cessna two two seven three, five miles east, at one thousand three hundred, landing runway one, Clearview." Kate looked at Jake. "How was that?"

"Clear and concise, Kate. Very good. Now let's keep looking for traffic."

Kate felt like she was flying one of the airliners she had watched land at San Jose from the mountaintop with her dad years ago.

"Clearville traffic, Cessna two two seven three turning downwind, runway one, Clearville."

Jake laughed. "Where's Clearville?"

Kate was momentarily confused, then realized her mistake.

"That's okay, kid, I murdered my callouts when I first started. Shake it off and continue."

Kate smiled as she turned downwind.

"All right, we're downwind, set your throttle at fifteen hundred rpm, then flaps ten degrees, and I'll read the Landing Checklist. Carb heat—on, mixture—rich, fuel—check."

Jake read aloud as Kate performed each task and responded.

"Okay, Kate, now slow to seventy, then set the flaps to twenty degrees."

As the craft slowed, Kate adjusted the trim while monitoring her descent rate.

"Perfect. Don't forget to call base."

Jake watched Kate's progress as she guided the plane through the pattern.

"Clearview traffic, Cessna two two seven three turning base, runway one, Clearview." Kate glanced at the runway, then the airspeed indicator, and again the runway, gauging just the right moment to start her turn.

"Clearview traffic, Cessna two two seven three turning final, runway one, Clearview."

Kate got goosebumps as she lined up with the runway center line. This was the part of the flight Kate loved the best: watching the runway grow ever larger.

"Very nice, now set flaps to forty degrees and trim the nose up to hold this speed," Jake instructed.

Kate had the approach nailed, on speed, on glide slope.

"Wait until we reach hangar height, then start bringing the nose up into the landing attitude as you stay lined up with the runway center line."

Jake placed his hand lightly on the controls, monitoring Kate's inputs, ready to intervene if needed. "That's it, Kate, nice and smooth on the controls, small inputs."

At this level of concentration, Kate excelled. Every fiber of her being was somehow part of the aircraft, laser-focused on the task at hand. She was ahead of the airplane, not just reacting.

"What's that!" she yelled. "There!"

Jake looked as Kate pushed the throttle all the way in, adding full power, and began reciting out loud, and performing the go-around procedure she had just learned.

"Power! Attitude!" Kate fought the growing force needed to keep the nose from rising too high. "Trim nose down! Positive rate of climb, flaps up twenty." Kate paused the flaps, allowing the plane's speed to build as she again adjusted the trim. "Flaps ten!"

"That's it, Kate, stay with it," Jake encouraged as he announced their departure.

"Carb heat off." Kate reached forward, again adjusting the trim, canceling the pressure needed to hold the nose just above the horizon. Jake followed lightly on the controls, knowing it was critical that every action be performed at just the right time, in just the right way.

Kate reacted instinctively, stabilizing the plane in a climb before glancing at Jake.

He smiled, "announce your turn to crosswind and that we're departing the pattern to the east, then we'll talk."

But Kate just sat there as what happened started to sink in.

"Okay, kiddo, just calm down and fly the plane. Take a deep breath." Jake hit his push-to-talk button and announced their intentions on the radio.

"Did you see those kids running out onto the runway?"

"Relax, you did great! Now climb up to two thousand and we'll set up again as soon as you're ready. And remember, no matter what happens, fly the plane."

"I can't believe it—they were right in front of us!" Kate declared, perplexed and a bit angry.

"Listen, kiddo, I never saw them, and suddenly you're going around." Jake chuckled. "That was amazing, you reacted perfectly. You're going to make a hell of a pilot, young lady!"

"Yeah, a pilot who almost peed her pants," Kate added, causing Jake to laugh harder.

168

After calming down, Kate returned to the airport and made an acceptable landing, but not before Jake had her go around again. Kate taxied up to the fuel pump, where Jake taught her how to refuel the Cessna, then accompanied her into the airport office to go over the day's events.

Kate was totally exhausted as she entered the office.

Michelle, who was sitting behind the counter, rose from her chair holding Kate's logbook.

"Hi, Mrs. Collins," Kate greeted. "Did you see the kids on the runway? We had to go around," she added in a grown-up tone.

"I know. The reason I looked out the window was that I heard you going to full power, and there in the middle of the runway I spotted three kids running as fast as they could toward this side of the airport."

"And then Jake sprang another aborted landing on me!"

Michelle looked over at Jake. "You're cruel."

"I'll take that as a compliment," Jake responded with a smile. "Did you catch them?"

"They were good kids, Jake. I just waved them over and explained things. They knew they screwed up."

"I hope you weren't too hard on them," Jake said, getting a drink from the water fountain.

"No, but as I said, I don't think they'll do that again." Michelle handed Jake Kate's logbook.

He walked over to the old table and had a seat. "Sit down with me, Kate. Let's fill this out together."

Crossroads

Chapter 17:
Staying Ahead of the Game

Frank, Susan, and Anna sat transfixed as Kate described in detail every facet of the day's flight.

"Relax, Anna," Frank cut in, reading the look of concern on her face. "Jake told me that an aborted landing is a normal procedure, and how impressed he was that Kate pulled it off after just learning it. Besides, Jake was never going to let things get out of hand, right?"

Poor Anna didn't know what to think at this point, and just shook her head.

After dinner, Frank suggested everyone walk off the meal, but Kate had other plans and stayed behind. As the grown-ups left, Kate went up to her room and brought down the book her father had picked up for her, *The Student Pilot's Flight Manual*. She sat at the kitchen table and opened it to the chapter on the national airspace system, and visual flight rules, known as VFR. Jake had been giving Kate ground school in the airport's computer room ever since she had returned, and Kate's new reading skills were allowing her to read chapters ahead of what Jake was teaching. She found that by reviewing the material first, she better understood everything Jake was teaching. The joke was that she never told Jake, leading him to believe that his student was a gifted child!

#

Kate had put her book away and was just hanging

up with Jess after talking with Bruce when the trio got back from their walk. "Mom, Bruce asked if he could drive me to the fair this weekend. You know, the same one we went to last year?"

Before Anna had time to say no, Sue interjected, "Kate, I'm picking up a new car this Friday evening, and I was hoping I could give everyone a ride to the fair on Saturday. You know, to break it in. Maybe we can meet him there?"

Although disappointed, Kate didn't want to spoil her aunt's plans and agreed to meet Bruce at the fair.

#

Sue guided her new Jeep Cherokee into the Napa Valley fairgrounds parking lot. Frank, who was riding shotgun, got out first and spotted Bruce waiting at the front gate. "How are you, Bruce?" Frank asked, giving the young man a firm handshake.

"I'm great, Mr. Wilson. Is that a new truck?"

"Yep, my wife just picked it up yesterday. Have you decided on what colleges you're thinking about, now that you're a senior?"

"I'm thinking Napa Valley College, sir. They have a great viticulture and winery program. I plan to stay in the valley and work at my family's vineyard."

"Congratulations, Bruce, that sounds like a wonderful idea."

"Good evening, Mrs. Wilson—and Mrs. Wilson and Miss Wilson," Bruce said, giving them a laugh. "You look nice, Kate."

"Thank you," Kate replied, slightly embarrassed,

but happy for the compliment. After entering the fairgrounds, Sue suggested Bruce and Kate go off and have fun, and that they would meet at that very spot at 9:30 p.m.

Anna couldn't help but linger for a moment, watching her little girl walk away with a young man at her side. Frank came over and put his arm around his sister-in-law, giving her a hug. "Come on, Mom, they're fine."

"Oh, I know that, I just can't believe she's grown up so fast."

With that, the three sauntered off in the direction of the 1960's tribute band Sue had read about.

Kate and Bruce, meanwhile, spent most of the evening talking and catching up. Bruce told Kate of his college plans, and Kate confessed that she was still undecided about what career path to follow.

"It sounds to me like you want to be a pilot, Kate. Have you thought about it?" Bruce asked as the two boarded the Ferris wheel. "I am thinking about that, but I have time to make up my mind, right?"

"Sure, it's not a race. I'm sure you'll make the right decision."

The two fell quiet as the Ferris wheel picked up speed, making several turns, before suddenly coming to a stop, with Kate and Bruce's gondola at the very top, rocking back and forth.

Startled, Kate grabbed Bruce's hand. He looked at her, leaned over, and kissed her on the lips. It was a tender kiss, not just a peck. The two smiled at each other as the Ferris wheel resumed moving. Kate was in a fog; she had wondered if Bruce would ever kiss her, and had dreamed about her first kiss for years. The wondering was over, and it was everything she'd hoped a first kiss would be. Kate slid closer to Bruce and held his hand tighter.

Frank sat in the front seat of his wife's new car, holding his ears as Anna and his wife shrieked, listening to Kate described what happened. Anna's eyes filled with tears (again), as did Sue's. There was a moment of silence, then the questions began. Frank just shook his head, quipping, "Just bury me," as he realized there was no escaping the conversation, or the punch in the arm Sue gave him for his remark.

At breakfast, Frank informed Kate of the day's chores. "Kate, if you feel up to it, I could use a hand down at the lower field."

"Sure thing, Uncle Frank, I love working in the fields."

"Great. We'll start the day pruning the vines, and then the irrigation system needs to be checked. So, after breakfast, you can take the tractor. I'll meet you there with the pickup after I grab a few tools from the garage."

"Sounds like a plan," Kate observed, as she dove into the pancakes her mom had just put in front of her.

"Paying Kate is very generous of you, Frank," Anna remarked, giving her brother-in-law a kiss on the cheek.

"Well, flying lessons cost money," Frank said, then began eating.

Frank had opened a savings account for Kate, making deposits appropriate to hours she worked (and then some), which Kate was using for her lessons.

Between flying lessons, working at the vineyard, and spending time with Bruce, she had a busy month. The days and weeks passed quickly that summer. Kate even started driving lessons with her uncle. Sticking to his military training, Frank began each driving lesson with a talk about what the mission was for that day, and the items he would be watching for.

"So...what is one of the most important things I have taught you so far, Kate?" Frank asked before setting out.

Kate smiled, knowing it was never one thing. "Brakes don't stop cars, people do."

"What else?"

"Keep an eye on your rearview mirror, and watch for aggressive drivers approaching from behind."

"And what else?

"Hit your four-way flashers if you see a sudden stoppage or accident up ahead, to wake up the drivers behind you."

"That's great sweetheart, let's go drive somewhere."

Kate could only smile.

Chapter 18:
A Cross-Country Adventure

Kate stood up from the table and stretched after her hour-and-a-half ground school lesson in the airport office's computer room. Its computer, internet access, and whiteboard were well suited for classroom instruction.

Besides learning about the different airspace rules and regulations, Kate was taught the phonetic alphabet or words used in place of letters, as radio static could result in letters like "A" and "J" being indistinguishable.

"All right, Kate, before you put your notebook away, I want you to write this down."

Jake waited a moment for Kate to sit, then rattled off airports and their navigation codes. "Clearview, Charlie Three One; Red Bluff, Romeo Bravo Lima; Colusa, Oscar Zero Eight; then back to Charlie Three One. Now that we've finished the lessons on VFR navigation and airspace, I want you to plan this flight, complete with everything you've learned. Flight times, fuel requirements, altitudes, everything. Let's plan it for this coming Saturday."

Kate was thrilled and spent the next few evenings planning the flight, drawing course lines on her chart, and highlighting landmarks. The evening before her flight, Anna and Sue presented Kate with a special cake in the shape of California to mark the occasion. After finishing his cake, Frank excused himself from the table, and promptly returned with a small package. "Here you go, Miss

Practically a Pilot."

Sue looked at her husband suspiciously. "What did you do?"

"Relax, it's something she could use."

Kate's face lit up. "Uncle Frank!" She held up a new pair of Ray-Ban Aviator sunglasses and immediately tried them on. "Oh my gosh, they're beautiful, Uncle Frank. Thank you!" Kate gave her uncle a big hug. "They're perfect."

"You're welcome, honey. Wear them in good health."

That night, Kate had trouble falling asleep but was up with the sun, already dressed and on the phone with Flight Service, getting her first weather briefing.

"How does it look, Kate?" Anna asked as she came in to start breakfast.

"Sunny all day, with light winds from the west, Mom. It looks like the perfect day!"

#

"Clear!" Kate yelled as the Mighty 150 roared to life.

"All right, Kate, it's all you today," Jake said, seated to her right. Kate inched the plane forward, testing the brakes, before taxiing to the runway. "I'm happy it's such a perfect day, Jake. I've been looking forward to this."

"I remember my first cross-country, missy. I got lost."

Kate spun her head. "Really?"—amazed that Jake could do anything wrong.

"Yep. I ended up seven miles south of my second

airport, and my instructor just sat there and watched it happen. I had to take a second cross-country flight with him before he would sign me off."

"So that's what I have to look forward to?"

"Nope. This is an instructional flight, and seeing as I'm the instructor I promise to make it fun and informative."

Kate smiled as her apprehension disappeared.

She departed the pattern on course and climbed through the crisp morning air toward her first destination, way out over the horizon. The first thing that struck Kate was how busy she was. There were so many things to attend to—altitude, heading, traffic, and reading the chart—but she took it all in stride. Kate saw her first landmark, Lake Berryessa, appreciating the stark beauty of the barren hills stretching out before her.

"This is a rough area, Jake; I would hate to have engine trouble around here."

"Yeah, not many flat areas to put it down. Let's climb up to seven thousand five hundred. That way we'll increase our glide range. And keep looking for good places to put it down. That's your spot until it's too far behind us, or you see a better one."

Kate never anticipated just how many tasks she would have to juggle, and now the uneven, hostile terrain added to the workload.

As she climbed, Kate felt her stress melting away as more favorable spots to land came into glide range. But then another situation developed, for up ahead Kate could see she was going to miss her next landmark by a few miles.

"Okay, missy, looks like we're drifting off course. What's the plan?"

"I'm going to correct my magnetic heading to compensate for the increased crosswind."

"Good, but your original course passes right over that lake, so first let's fly to the lake, and then turn to your new magnetic heading."

"Is that how you got lost on your first cross-country?"

"Yep. Instead of flying over to the known landmark, I just added a few degrees to my heading and kept going. From that point on, things just didn't look right. I missed my destination by seven miles."

As the flight continued, Kate kept busy, monitoring her progress and recording her time between landmarks. Then she took a moment and smiled. She was finally piloting an aircraft to a distant destination, and having the time of her life!

"Traffic at ten o'clock."

Jake's voice snapped Kate out of her romantic trance and back into pilot mode. "There." Jake pointed to a twin-engine aircraft slicing through the air, a mile out in front, and slightly above the two aviators. Kate, realizing there was no conflict, watched as the plane grew smaller as it raced off to the east.

"Kate, I was taught to aim at the tail and forget it," Jake remarked, seeing his student fixated on the twin.

"I don't understand."

"Look, kiddo, if you encounter crossing traffic, just

aim at the tail and forget it. It's fun watching it fly away, but you might get hit by one you didn't see."

Kate made a mental note and got back to work.

As the Cessna cleared the hills, Kate could make out the north–south interstate off in the distance, which led directly to Red Bluff, her first airport. Jake had been hoping for a hazy day to reduce visibility and make navigation more challenging. However, he would not be disappointed in the arrival to Red Bluff as a learning opportunity.

At twenty-five miles from their first destination, Jake had Kate tune the radio to Red Bluff's frequency, to get an idea of the traffic in the area. What the pair heard was not the quiet hiss usually encountered, which occasionally interrupted by an arriving or departing aircraft. What they did hear sent a shiver down Kate's spine.

"Red Bluff traffic, experimental three miles north of the junkyard, for downwind runway three three, Red Bluff."

"Red Bluff traffic, Cessna turning base runway three three, Red Bluff."

"Red Bluff traffic, Baron clear of three three, Red Bluff."

"Red Bluff traffic, Bonanza three miles to the west, headed to the junkyard, we'll swing north, how fast is that experimental?"

"One twenty for the experimental, already over the junkyard."

"Okay, thanks, we're slowing down, Bonanza now

two miles west, we have the traffic, we'll be turning downwind over the junk yard for three three, Red Bluff."

"Red Bluff traffic..."

Kate and Jake looked at each other as planes continued calling in.

"Wow, looks like something big is going on today," Jake offered as Kate stared back with the same look she'd had after she was first forced to go around.

"All right, kiddo, let's just keep listening to what's going on so we can paint a mental picture of the traffic in the area. If it's still a beehive when we're seven miles out, we'll just park and wait until things calm down."

Kate gave Jake a puzzled look. "How do you park an airplane in the air?"

"We'll just find a quiet piece of sky and orbit until we feel comfortable, then we'll go in. That way we mitigate the risk of arriving when it's really busy."

Kate laughed and shook her head, amazed at the simplicity of the plan, and how much she had already learned today.

She listened for a few minutes. Pilots were entering the downwind leg from a junkyard, filled with old cars, just north of the field.

"I see the wheels spinning in your head, Kate. Have you come up with a plan yet?"

"Well, everyone is approaching the airport from the north, using that junkyard as a reporting point. Since we're approaching from the south, how about we divert our course to the west, well clear of the traffic pattern? When we're northwest of the airport, we can fly to the junkyard and enter downwind, like everyone else."

"Good job, Kate, that's exactly what I would do. Let's start our descent to three thousand so we can stay above the arriving traffic. You can announce ten miles out, and let people know your intentions, so think about what you're going to say, and keep your transmissions short and to the point."

Kate began descending as she thought about what she would say. A few minutes later, once level at three thousand feet and ten miles south, Kate keyed the mic. "Red Bluff traffic, Cessna two two seven three, ten miles south, three thousand feet, passing Red Bluff, west of the interstate, Red Bluff."

Her heartbeat picked up as the airport came into view off to her right while they listened to the position reports coming in from arriving aircraft.

Kate could see the airport and what looked to be a large parking lot a mile north of the field. "That's the junkyard."

"I agree. Now let's descend to pattern altitude and start a wide right turn. I'll handle the radio for you."

"Red Bluff traffic, Cessna three miles north, descending out of three thousand turning south for the junkyard, landing three three, Red Bluff."

Kate completed her turn toward the junkyard, leveling off at pattern altitude at the same time, and immediately called out traffic.

"Biplane, eleven o'clock."

Jake looked to the left and spotted a yellow and blue Stearman at their altitude, about a half mile in front of them moving left to right, and headed for the junkyard. Kate leaned forward in her seat, placing her right hand on the dash, pulling herself forward in an attempt to see better as she aimed at his tail while looking left, making sure no planes were behind it.

"What's this?" Jake said, taking her hand and moving it back to the throttle. "Don't get all tense on me now, just relax, you're doing great. This is perfect, Kate. Fall in behind him. I'll report that we're falling in behind the Stearman. That plane is easy to identify and other planes should have no problem knowing where we are, but you can't fly leaning forward like that, just relax and fly the plane. That Stearman probably doesn't have a radio, that's why he came out of nowhere."

Kate fell in, well behind the blue/yellow target, and began her Landing Checklist as Jake, still scanning for traffic, made radio calls and reminded her to extend her downwind to give the biplane time to land and clear the runway.

Kate was again absorbed in the task at hand. She loved that she was flying behind another airplane and could actually make out control surfaces moving on the wings and tail. It was amazing to watch as the two crafts seemed to float along. And it was a Stearman, of all things, painted the same colors as one she had seen overhead so long ago.

Everything was going great until Kate turned final, toward the runway.

"What's that on the apron?" she asked, seeing what looked like a crowded mall parking lot the day before

Christmas.

"Just concentrate on landing right now, missy. There's a plane entering downwind, so I want to see a nice landing on the numbers and a smart exit off the runway."

Kate was on her game and made an excellent landing, despite her nerves.

"Great job, Kate. Now let's just taxi off onto the grass. This is a fly-in, so there might be a lot of people walking around. There should be linesmen showing you were to park—look for the red or yellow vest. Remember, you're the pilot, so don't do anything you're uncomfortable with, just move cautiously."

Kate's heart raced even faster. People walking around? A fly-in? Really!

She quickly realized that the situation was not as dire as she first feared. Men with yellow vests, holding red batons, waved her forward and directed her to a parking spot, as other men kept people well clear of moving aircraft.

Kate, however, held her breath as a linesman standing in front of her parking spot motioned her forward until he crossed his batons.

Kate shut down, happy she hadn't run the man over. Leg one of her first cross-country complete!

"You did it, Kate. Nice job!"

"Wow, is this some kind of party or something?"

"Let's get out and secure the aircraft, and I'll explain it to you, Miss Aviator."

Kate stopped for a moment; Jake had never said that to her before. No one had ever called her that. What

184

a day this was turning out to be!

Even before Kate had placed chocks against the wheels, onlookers started asking questions about where they had flown in from, and if Kate had indeed been flying the airplane.

"Let's take a walk, kiddo," Jake said with a smile once things quieted down.

"Jake, what is this?"

"The local EAA chapter here at Red Bluff is holding a fly-in this weekend. Basically pilots fly in from all over the state for lunch, and to meet with friends. At some fly-ins, they even award trophies to the best-looking aircraft in different categories."

Kate couldn't get over the number of different airplanes parked on the apron, or the fact that the event was open to the public, which explained all the kids. Arriving at the open hangar, she realized it was not just a spur-of-the-moment gathering. Inside the hangar, rows of tables and chairs were occupied by people eating lunch, talking, and having a good time.

Jake directed Kate to the registration desk, where he signed both of them in. The pair learned that a photographer had been stationed at the approach end of the runway taking pictures of arriving aircraft, all of which would later be posted on a webpage.

Kate loved the idea that her first cross-country might be documented in a picture. "Come on, kiddo, let's get some lunch," Jake said, removing his wallet.

"Not so fast, Jake, this is my treat," Kate insisted, stepping in front and paying before Jake could protest.

185

The big man stepped back and smiled. "Thank you, missy."

"It's my pleasure, Mr. Jake," Kate replied with a smile. Jake smiled, shaking his head.

As the pair stood in line, people stopped to say hello to Jake, one after the other. At one point there were three men waiting to speak with him. *Wow, Jake is a rock star*, Kate thought with a smile as she took it all in. Then she heard Jake remark that he had followed this man in.

Suddenly it hit her!

"Wait!" Kate blurted.

Both men stopped and looked at her.

"Oh my gosh, I'm so sorry for interrupting, but were you flying the blue and yellow biplane?"

"Yes, I was, miss. Dan Preston, pleased to meet you," the pilot answered, shaking Kate's hand.

"I'm so pleased to meet you, sir. I'm Kate Wilson, Jake's student. Have you ever flown over Los Angeles?"

Dan looked at Kate, puzzled. "Yes, I did, but not since April two years ago."

Kate just stared for a moment and felt as if she was in a play, or was it all a conspiracy? No, it couldn't be.

"I saw you, it was evening," was all she could get out.

Dan smiled. "Yes, when I landed. Well, I guess my airplane made an impression on you! I'm so happy you remembered." Dan looked back at Jake. "Buddy, I've got to run, it's great seeing you again."

Dan looked at Kate. "Young lady, the pleasure has been all mine, best of luck to you."

186

And with that, he was gone.

Jake noticed that Kate was unusually quiet while they ate. "What's going on, missy?" he finally asked.

Kate smiled. "I can't believe I met the pilot of the plane that flew over me. My girlfriend Jess is never going to believe me."

"Well, aviation is a small community of very nice people. As you go along, you're going to find that this sort of thing happens all the time. Heck, half the people I've met today, I haven't seen in twenty years."

Kate just smiled.

After a wonderful lunch, and some homemade ice cream, the pair strolled the flight line. As they walked, Kate asked about the different types of aircraft, listening intently as Jake explained their different flying characteristics and manufacturing techniques. After an hour, Jake and Kate returned to their airplane and prepared to depart.

"How are we ever going to get out of here with all these people around?"

"You untie the plane, I'll go round up a couple of linesmen," Jake suggested. "They'll take care of the crowds, and help pull the airplane out as far as we can, before starting up."

After taxiing out, Kate lined up behind other departures, all heading for different corners of the state. "Geez, it looks like we're number five to depart."

"You'll be surprised how quickly things move along when the pattern is clear," Jake responded. "Just remember, Kate, there is no rushing in aviation. We depart only when you're ready."

After taking off from Red Bluff, Kate struck out on the next leg of the cross-country. "You did a great job getting out of there, Kate. We'll make up some time at Colusa by landing and just taking off again."

As they flew south toward Colusa, Kate asked if Red Bluff was the biggest fly-in he had ever been to. Jake smiled as if reliving fond memories. "Well, Kate, the largest fly-in on the planet happens next week in Oshkosh, Wisconsin. It's called AirVenture and is the home of the EAA. For seven days and nights, Wittman Regional Airport becomes the busiest airport in the entire world, with thousands of airplanes flying in and parking, and thousands of people camping on the airport grounds."

Kate grinned, trying to imagine the scene. "What do people do there? Is it like the fly-in we just left?"

"Much bigger, Kate. There are air shows every day, and huge pavilions filled with vendors selling everything aviation. They even have forums where you can get your hands dirty learning the same skills you and the other students are using on the school plane. There's fabric covering, welding, and riveting, which are skills you'll need to learn while building your own airplane. Vintage planes, warbirds, they're all there."

Kate was amazed. How was is it that no one knew about this? Then suddenly a thought. "Jake, I want to fly to AirVenture one of these days."

He laughed. "Okay, girl, hold your horses. It's a long ride from here to Oshkosh unless you're thinking about flying commercially."

188

"No, I want to fly an airplane and land. Everything you've told me about AirVenture sounds so amazing."

"Yeah, well, remember this, missy. If you thought getting into Red Bluff was tricky, wait till you get to Oshkosh."

"Why, is it dangerous?"

"No, it's very organized. In fact, they publish a pamphlet called a NOTAM, or Notice to Airmen, that lays out what pilots have to do to orchestrate the orderly arrival of so many aircraft. But it's not for the faint of heart. I have an old AirVenture arrival NOTAM that you can have, and you can go online and take a look at videos from past AirVenture fly-ins."

"Now I really want to go!" Kate said, smiling.

It didn't take long for the little Cessna to fly south along the highway to Colusa. After touching down, Kate taxied back to the departure end of the runway, reconfigured the aircraft for takeoff, and departed toward the final leg of their journey.

As Kate guided the plane west toward Clearview, she observed a change in the weather up ahead. Clouds were coming in off the ocean, and the wind had picked up, causing the plane to bounce around.

"Looks like we're in for some turbulence, Kate. How are you going to handle it?"

Kate looked at her instruments. "The green arc on the airspeed indicator is the maneuvering speed, which is slow enough to protect the airframe, so I'll make sure I keep the speed in the green."

"That's good, Kate. We can also slow it down even

more, so these bumps don't bang us around too much, and tighten up that lap belt while you're at it."

The turbulence intensified, and Kate struggled to hold her altitude as the small plane dropped and climbed.

"Jake, my airspeed is all over the place."

Jake laughed as he snatched his pen in midair before it had a chance to fall. "Yeah, they sure missed this forecast. Kate, don't chase your airspeed. Keep a level attitude and let the plane fall and rise with the air currents. And reduce power. Let's descend and see if we can find smoother air."

Kate held steady, letting the airspeed and altitude fluctuate. At one point, the stall warning horn actually chirped before things started calming down.

"Today we'll have a direct crosswind on landing, so remember, it's your track over the ground that counts," Jake advised. "Don't worry about how the plane is facing, just crab as necessary. Before touchdown, kick out the crab with rudder. It's okay to touch down on one wheel; the other wheel will come down a moment later, you just stay on that center line."

"I remember Jake. We had to do that three weeks ago, and I kind of enjoyed the challenge, remember?"

"That's right. If you're going to fly, you've got to know how to fly in the wind."

The rest of the flight was not much fun. The wind made Kate feel as if she was sailing a small boat in an angry sea. However, the excitement of entering the pattern, and the challenge of a crosswind landing, made any fatigue she might have felt disappear.

190

Kate entered the pattern flying the downwind leg for runway one from the east, the west wind reducing her ground speed by fifteen knots. Kate smiled, loving the challenge, which only added to her sense of adventure. To fly parallel to the runway, Kate held the nose of the plane close to thirty degrees into the wind, sliding along the downwind leg with the airport at her eight o clock as the wind tried to push her off course.

"This is a good time to take a look at the windsock and see what the wind is like on the ground," Jake said.

Kate took a good look. "It looks like eight or nine miles per hour, but sometimes it's straight out, and it looks like it's out of the northwest."

"I agree. What does that do to your approach speed on final?"

"I'm going to add ten miles per hour and approach at eighty."

"That sounds like a good plan. Be ready with the throttle."

Kate added a little left bank entering the base leg, then turned final, holding a twenty-degree crab to the left. Just before touching down, she straightened out with right rudder. But she was a bit fast and ballooned for a moment before coming down with a mild crunch. Jake made light of the bounced landing, but Kate was upset. Once out of the airplane, Kate began to apologize.

Jake cut her off. "Look, kiddo, learning how to fly has plateaus, successes, and rough spots. Sure, you bounced the landing, but it wasn't all that bad, and this little trainer was designed for just such occasions. So let's put a smile on your face before we get into the office. You did great, and you'll find that no matter how many hours you've flown, you'll still bounce one now and then. Oh, and nice sunglasses."

Kate stopped and looked at Jake. "You just noticed?" She smiled, brushed off the landing, and went into the office wearing a smile.

An hour later, Kate was reliving the entire experience with her mother, aunt, and uncle as they drove home from the airport.

"Kate, call your dad, he's dying to hear about your flight."

"Sure thing, Mom. Oh, and I told Jake about Dad coming up to pick you up next Saturday."

"That's good, dear. What did he say when you told him?" Anna asked.

"He just smiled and said, 'Good timing,' but I didn't get it," Kate replied, before calling her father and her friend Jess.

Chapter 19:
A Day to Remember

The next Saturday at precisely 9:30, Kate pulled into the Clearview Airport parking lot, her uncle at her side. "Have a great lesson, Kate," Frank said as he switched seats.

"Jake warned me that I'll be here almost all day, Uncle Frank, so I'll call when I'm ready to be picked up. I know Dad left early; I'm sure he'll be here by then."

"All right, honey, we'll wait for your call."

As promised, Jake gave Kate a real workout, including a simulated forced landing and unusual attitudes. After two hours of instruction, and refueling, the pair headed off to the diner for lunch. Chris was at the cash register, and as the two aviators entered, Jake handed Chris a note, which she hurriedly read before putting into her pocket.

Once again, the Mighty 150 blasted off, but instead of heading for the practice area, Jake had Kate remain in the pattern, where he had her perform a soft-field and short-field landing, aborted takeoff, and a go around. Jake looked at his watch and then did something Kate never saw coming. After the aircraft turned off the runway, Jake asked Kate to stop on the taxiway and shut down.

Kate was confused as Jake checked the fuel gauges. "Okay, missy, it's time."

"Time for what?"

"It's time you take this plane up by yourself."

Kate's heart skipped a beat as Jake continued in his usual nonchalant way.

"Don't do anything stupid, just take off, fly the pattern, and land. I'll be waiting for you at the tie-down."

Kate didn't say a word as Jake unbuckled and got out of the plane, then turned and secured the seat belt. "She's gonna get off the ground real quick without me in there, and she'll climb a lot faster. Don't let that scare you, just do what you did all day and you'll be fine. Okay?"

The best that Kate could manage was a thumbs-up. Jake gave her a wink, closed the door, and walked away. *Heck, he didn't even stick around to see if I remembered how to start the darn thing!*

Kate took a deep breath, opened the side window, looked around, and yelled as loud as she could, "Clear!"

As the engine roared back to life, Kate checked the gauges and began another chapter in her life.

The Mighty 150's prop wash shook the plane as Kate looked around for any other ground traffic, then announced she was taxiing for takeoff from one niner.

At the run-up area, Kate took a moment, going over the flight in her head, before starting the Pre-Takeoff Checklist.

Cabin doors—latched. Flight controls—free and correct. Elevator trim—takeoff position. Carb heat—off. Mixture—full rich.

She was ready!

"Clearview traffic, Cessna two two seven three departing runway one niner, closed circuit, Clearview."

194

Unbeknown to Kate, her family had been watching from the office as Jake walked away from the plane. Chris was watching from the hangar, still holding the note Jake had given her, which read: "Call Frank, Kate's going to solo, be here at 2:45 and remain out of sight until she takes off."

In the plane, Kate looked toward the north for traffic on long final, then taxied onto the center of the runway and stopped. She listened to the hum of the engine as she watched the propeller turn, knowing it was a moment in her life she would never forget.

Looking down the runway, Kate felt the white lines beckoning her forward. After a quick glance at the oil pressure, and a steady push on the throttle, the Mighty 150 surged forward, racing down the runway. Kate instinctively used the rudder to stay over the white lines, then in mere seconds she was up, climbing away, faster than ever before. With less weight the small plane climbed faster, and flew differently, quicker, nimbler, throwing off Kate's timing.

"Clearview traffic, Cessna two two seven three turning crosswind, closed circuit, one niner, Clearview."

Kate was uneasy about how fast things were happening, and how different it felt to not have her instructor there to reassure her. The small plane climbed like a homesick angel, resulting in a shorter and more hurried pattern. "Clearview traffic, Cessna two two seven three turning downwind one niner, Clearview."

"Okay, pattern altitude. Just take care of business!" Kate said out loud to collect herself. "All right, let's slow it down!"

But just as Kate reached for the throttle, the plane's right wing dropped...turbulence...maybe a thermal rising from the ground, whatever it was, Kate felt like she was all over the sky. It felt like a different plane, but she refused to acknowledge the panic that nipped at her, choosing instead to calm herself down out loud. "Easy does it, girl, don't overcontrol! Calm down!" She took a deep breath. "Slow down, dammit!"

Kate backed off the throttle and held her altitude as the plane decelerated. Finally things started to fall into place. Kate grabbed the Landing Checklist, getting ready to land as she pulled carb heat and continued on downwind.

Once abeam her touchdown point, Kate moved the flap handle to ten degrees.

Maybe it was the added drag or the familiar whirring of the flap motors welcoming her home. Or maybe it was just plain-old confidence, born of thorough preparation. Whatever it was, Kate was back!

"Okay, you got this!" Kate said, smiling.

"Clearview traffic, Cessna two two seven three turning base one niner, Clearview."

Kate looked to her right for planes on long final while she managed her airspeed and gauged her descent.

"Clearview traffic, Cessna two two seven three turning final, runway one niner, Clearview."

"Okay, flaps forty, trim for seventy, now just sit here and wait." Kate had it all together, steady as a rock, as she anticipated the afternoon's bumpy air, feeding in corrections before the little plane even twitched.

"Okay, seventy and on glide slope, runway is clear, feet off the brakes."

As always, this was the part of the pattern she loved, watching the runway grow, frozen in the windshield. It was thrilling!

Everyone on the ground watched intently as the little plane turned toward the runway. Jake, arms folded, stood and watched, confident in his student's ability.

"Okay, get ready," Kate said as she added back pressure to the yoke, transitioning to landing attitude. "Look far," she reminded herself, adjusting her gaze from her aim point to the end of the runway. "Back off the power, get the nose up, okay, settle, settle, hold it off, hold it off."

With barely a chirp, Kate rolled the plane onto the runway. A greaser!

"Holy mackerel, I did it!" Kate shouted as she rolled out, gently bringing the Cessna to a crawl, and turning onto the taxiway.

As happy as Kate was, she couldn't help but feel a bit let down that her family wouldn't be here to help celebrate. But boy, she couldn't wait to call her dad.

Kate made the turn onto the ramp, watching that her right wingtip cleared the tall bushes, then looked forward and burst into tears.

They were here!

Her dad was here!

Everyone was standing near the office—her father, mother, aunt, and uncle, all clapping. Chris and Michelle were also clapping. Jake simply grinned. Kate shut down and got out of the plane and ran into her father's and mother's arms. Chris gave Jake a pat on the back. "Good job, honey. Another Young Eagle has left the nest."

Jake quickly wiped his eye and turned toward her. "Hell, she was ready last week. I just wanted the parents to surprise her after she landed."

"Dad, I'm so happy you're here!"

Kate's dad looked at Chris as he wiped a tear from his eye. "Chris gave us the heads-up, honey. We watched from the office as Jake got out of the plane. We saw the whole thing! Your mom was so nervous I thought she was going to break!"

Michelle came forward and called Jake over to where Kate was standing. "Congratulations, Kate, on your first solo. Now, keeping with tradition, Jake has a ceremonial function to perform before your solo is official."

Kate's family stood back as Michelle handed Jake a Magic Marker and pair of scissors then stepped back and gave him some room.

"It looked like you hit a few bumps on downwind."

"I know. I felt like I was all over the sky!"

"Didn't look that way from the ground, missy, you did great. Now turn around, kiddo, I promise this won't hurt a bit."

Kate remembered the pieces of cloth hanging in the office hall, each commemorating the date and time a flight student soloed. Smiling, Kate spun and pulled the back of her shirt out for Jake. "Thanks, kid." He laughed as he used a black marker to write Kate's name and the date in large print, and proceeded to cut that portion from the back of Kate's shirt. Everyone clapped as Jake took the liberated fabric and shook it above his head. Kate gave Jake a hug. "Thank you for everything, Jake."

"Don't thank me yet, missy. The work has just begun."

Everyone followed Michelle into the office, where she took the fabric and read it out loud before stapling it to the office wall.

Bob tapped on a coffee mug to get everyone's attention. "Anna and I would be honored if everyone joined us for dinner at Folino's this evening. We have reservations for 6:30 and would love if you could come and help us celebrate Kate's big day."

That evening, the server at Folino's had just finished delivering drinks when Kate looked up to see Bruce walking in, holding flowers!

"Sorry I'm late, Mr. and Mrs. Wilson, I just finished up." Anna nudged Sue to look up. This was the first time Kate had received flowers from a young man.

"Congratulations, Fly Girl!" Bruce said. He bent over and gave Kate a peck on the lips before presenting her with the bouquet. Anna smiled, Bob stood to shake Bruce's hand, and Sue gave Frank a soft shot in the arm. "Hey," he said. "What was that for?"

"That's for never buying me flowers."

Frank laughed. "You haven't soloed yet."

"Watch it, buster," she retorted with a smile as everyone rose to shake Bruce's hand.

That evening, Anna followed her daughter up to

her bedroom to tuck her in one last time before heading back home with Bob.

"I loved spending July here with you, Kate, and Bruce is such a nice boy. I hope the two of you enjoy the bowling date he told me about this evening."

"Thanks, Mom. I can't believe he bought me flowers. That's the first time I ever got flowers from a boy!"

"I know, dear. I gave your aunt Susan a nudge when I saw Bruce come in with them. We both had a tear in our eye. Honey, Dad and I are so proud of you. Please be careful flying around by yourself! And don't take any chances, and call me after every lesson! Promise me!"

"Mom, of course, I'll be careful. What's going on?"

Tears began running down Anna's face. Surprised, Kate sat up and held her mother close. "Mom, what's the matter?"

"I'm sorry, honey, you're growing up so fast, and now you're flying planes and driving tractors. It just seems like it's too soon."

Kate's own eyes teared up as she held her mother. "Mom, I love you more than anything in the world. I promise after this summer I won't grow anymore."

Anna laughed and hugged Kate as hard as she could. "Well, you can grow a little. Just promise me that you're never getting into a rocket. I never know what to expect from you!"

Anna dried her eyes and gave Kate a kiss before going downstairs.

Kate put her head on the pillow, remembering the

night she'd cried herself to sleep in this same room. *A lot of water under the bridge*, she thought.

As she drifted off, she could almost see the runway dropping away.

Chapter 20:
Surprise

Kate pushed back from her desk, having just finished up a reading assignment, and sat quietly looking at the picture of herself and Jake landing at Red Bluff. Kate's junior year was half over and going great. Her improved reading skills, and judicial use of her cell phone, made schoolwork more manageable than ever. August was spent flying solo and learning radio navigation with Jake. Thanksgiving was again spent at the vineyard, where Bruce and Kate got a chance to catch up, and she flew with Jake, practicing radio navigation and operating in controlled airspace before flying solo around her practice area. As usual, the flight lessons were all business. Jake had her landing at towered airports, getting her used to the proper phraseology and following ATC instructions.

Kate's practice area was the same Jake had assigned her last August, an area thirty miles by thirty miles, with airports at the boundaries that could be used as alternate landing locations if weather moved into the Napa region.

Christmas vacation turned out to be very special, as Bruce and his family visited the Wilsons. The two families spent the week in LA taking movie studio tours, and visiting the Getty art museum along with the California Science Center. The two families got along great, and, best of all, Kate got to spend time with Bruce.

Now it was January and everyone in school was back in the groove. The RANS S-7 was in great shape. Three more students had joined the ranks of the build team, the plane was covered and being painted, and a benefactor had come forward providing the engine and agreeing to buy the aircraft after it was completed. The color scheme, voted on by the student body, was a deep yellow top and white bottom, separated by a two-inch-wide black accent stripe running along the sides, and along the wing.

There was much speculation among the students about the identity of the aircraft's new owner, which made the upcoming school assembly that much more exciting, as the owner's identity would finally be revealed. Kate thought for sure it was Mr. Rice.

After homeroom, Kate and Jess made their way down to the auditorium for the big announcement.

"What's so special about this airplane engine?" Jess asked as the two girls walked.

"It was built in Austria and is very reliable," Kate answered, holding the door for Jess.

"Well, one thing's for sure," Jess whispered as the pair entered the auditorium. "I'm going to make sure I know everything about the bugger."

Kate looked at her friend. "Why?"

"Because John has been working on the plane, and I understand that he's all excited about its engine, and I need something to talk to him about at the dance next weekend."

"Now I understand, you sneaky little thing," Kate

whispered. Both girls giggled.

Kate made sure they sat right in front of John, just to torture her friend, who in return kept pinching Kate's leg.

Kate looked at the stage and leaned over to Jess. "Boy, this must be a big deal, judging by the number of people on the stage."

The school's principal, vice principal, and PTO president, along with Mr. Rice and Mr. McDonnell, were all seated. Kate even noticed what she assumed was a reporter, complete with camera, standing off to the side.

After the Pledge of Allegiance and the singing of the school song, Mrs. Lamb, the vice principal, came to the microphone to introduce and thank everyone before handing the program over to Mr. Rice.

"Thank you, Mrs. Lamb, and good morning, students. As most of you know, our school aircraft is almost complete. This project would not have been possible without the support of the school administration and PTO along with the Build-A-Plane organization and of course the members of the EAA. And thank you to all the students on our aircraft build team. I'm so proud of everyone. I'm told by our EAA tutors that the workmanship performed by our student aircraft builders is first-class."

Mr. Rice searched the crowd for someone as he waited for the applause to end.

The moment didn't go unnoticed by Kate as she stood clapping, and she found it strange that his gaze stopped right at her.

204

"Now, as you all know, the biggest stumbling block to our successful completion of this project has been securing funds for the Rotax aircraft engine to power our bird. And finding someone seemed almost impossible until last week. But to bring you the details of this exciting development, I once again take great pleasure in introducing our lead construction supervisor, the president of EAA Chapter 1, Mr. Bob McDonnell."

Everyone clapped as Bob came to the microphone. "Boys and girls, I first have to thank your principal, Mr. Somo; the vice principal, Mrs. Lamb; and the PTO president, Mrs. Kirshner, for their support. And of course, none of this would have happened without your teacher and private pilot, Mr. Don Rice. He deserves a special thank-you for bringing the Build-A-Plane Program to your school. Aviation plays a very big role in our nation's economy. From employment opportunities to strategic national importance, the United States leads the world in aviation. And general aviation is its cornerstone. I'm happy to announce that the RANS aircraft project is right on schedule, and the FAA registration call sign, November one three three Charlie Victor, which stands for "Center Valley Might," has been assigned to your S-7 Courier."

Again everyone clapped.

"And now the big news. I am happy to announce that one of the biggest stumbling blocks to completing your aircraft has been overcome, thanks to the next gentleman I have the pleasure to introduce. Not only is he providing the funds to purchase the Rotax 912S one-hundred-horsepower engine. He has also agreed to purchase the aircraft after it has completed its inspection and phase one testing. So without further ado, please stand and give a big welcome to Mr. Frank Wilson."

Kate looked at Jess. "Frank Wilson? There's another Frank Wilson?"

Kate stood as she heard the name but couldn't comprehend what was happening, even after her uncle walked out onto the stage. Everyone was clapping, all except for Kate, that is. She just stood there and watched as her uncle shook everyone's hands and waved to the students.

Mr. Rice stepped to the mic and looked directly at Kate. "Would Kate Wilson please come up onto the stage?"

Jess looked at her. "Kate, he wants you to go up there."

Kate, still perplexed, squeezed past a few students and walked up on stage, wearing an uncertain smile. Frank met her at the top of the steps and gave her a big hug.

"Hi, Kate. Surprise!"

"What's happening, Uncle Frank? You bought the airplane?"

"I'll explain in a moment, kiddo, but first, turn around and look over to your left."

Kate spun to the left, and there next to the curtain stood the tall man who had taught her so much. Jake smiled and gave a little wave when Kate made eye contact with him.

Mr. Rice continued, "All right, let me have your attention, please. If you can all take your seats. As you have figured out by now, Mr. Wilson is our own Kate Wilson's uncle. Kate has been taking flying lessons for the past few years in Napa Valley while spending summers at her uncle's vineyard. Her uncle Frank came up with the idea of buying the plane to help Kate get the flight hours she needs as she pursues an aviation career, and now we have an even bigger surprise for all students. Especially all those who have worked so hard building the RANS. But to tell you about it, please give a warm welcome to Kate's flight instructor, Mr. Jake Hollerman."

Again the students stood and applauded.

Jake walked out onto the stage. "Come on, missy, stand next to me, you're going to love this." Kate looked at Jake, still stunned.

Jake took the mic from Mr. Rice and walked over to Kate. "You'll have to excuse Kate; she didn't know anything about this. You see, last year while on her first dual cross-country flight, Kate learned about the largest gathering of airplanes that occurs every summer in Oshkosh, Wisconsin. The event is called AirVenture, where for seven days Wittman Airport in Oshkosh becomes the busiest airport in the world, attracting over ten thousand aircraft and almost six hundred thousand people. It's the biggest air show and aviation event on the planet. I understand that the RANS will be flying by late May, and flight testing completed by early July. I'm happy to announce that Kate Wilson and I will be flying your plane to AirVenture!"

Everyone clapped as Kate looked up at Jake, then spun and looked at her uncle, not believing her ears. She was going to fly to Oshkosh!

Jake leaned over. "Besides doing most of the flying, Kate, you're going to handle all navigation, and fly the arrival procedure into the airport."

Mr. Rice came forward and again addressed the students. "Thank you, Jake. And now for the really big news. We have a go-ahead from the school administration, and parents of students on the build team, to announce that at the end of July a school trip is being planned to AirVenture in Oshkosh, Wisconsin."

The students jumped to their feet clapping and cheering!

"We're working with several airlines and hotels in an effort to secure low fares for everyone, and the trip will be open to all students and families."

It took a while for things to calm down before Mr. Rice could continue.

"I also wanted to tell you that Mr. McDonnell spoke with the folks at EAA headquarters and arranged for your aircraft to participate in the Homebuilts in Review, where homebuilt, or in this case *school* built, airplanes parade through the air in front of thousands of spectators."

Again everyone clapped, including Kate.

The applause continued as everyone on stage congratulated one another and posed for pictures.

Kate was still on stage when the assembly was dismissed, and smiled upon seeing Jess and John talking as they filed out. After the program, Kate was given permission to meet for lunch with her uncle and instructor.

"I guess I have a lot of studying to do in the next few months," she said.

"Yes, you do, missy, and I have a copy of this year's arrival procedure with me, so you can get a head start. You know, like last summer, when you read the flight manual before I gave the lesson." Kate laughed, realizing she was busted. Jake just gave her a knowing smile and handed her the pamphlet.

Kate, still processing the day, looked at her uncle. "Who came up with this idea?"

"Jake and I had lunch a few weeks ago, when I remembered you telling me about not having an engine for the school plane. When Jake told me about you having to rent the plane to fly solo and for the rest of your lessons, and of your desire to fly into the airshow, I got the idea that you can use the plane, and then when you're finished with it I'll sell it. The school trip to Oshkosh was Mr. Rice's idea, as a good way to keep students interested in aviation."

"I still can't believe it!" Kate smiled.

On the school bus that afternoon, Kate answered questions all the way home, with more from her mom when she arrived.

"How did it go today?" Anna asked, smiling, as her daughter came into the apartment. Kate ran over to her and gave her a big hug. "I still can't believe it, Mom," Kate stated as she relived the surprise. Bob arrived home from work sporting a huge grin. "Dad, I guess you already heard," Kate yelled as she ran over to give him a kiss.

"Heck, I knew about it for weeks, honey. See, I can keep a secret."

"That's because I grabbed the AirVenture brochure he left out on the table the other night," Anna chimed in.

"And that's why I love you, dear," Bob quipped, giving her a kiss hello.

# # #

Winter and early spring seemed to go by in a flash, with the delivery of a brand-new engine and instruments. Now it was May, and a new excitement filled the school halls when the aircraft's final assembly was completed. Center Valley High School's plane was finished!

On the second Saturday in May, build team students and parents gathered in the shop, in front of the plane the students had labored on for almost two years.

Mr. Rice and Bob McDonnell quieted everyone down and asked the student weight and balance committee to come up and start their job. Students placed scales in front of each main tire and pulled the plane up onto them. Then they raised the tail to cruise attitude using a support to hold it on a third scale.

"All right, team," Bob instructed. "Record the weight on each scale and fill out the form you have, as I explain what's going on to your parents."

Bob held up a model plane supported by a single cord attached to one of several hooks on top of the model.

"Now that the plane is complete, we have to make sure it is balanced according to the plans. The students are calculating the spot where the plane would hang perfectly level if hung by a rope. This point is called the center of gravity, or CG. Through the calculations the students are making, we will find the CG and establish the aircraft's loading limitation. The plane can safely fly as long as the CG stays within a few inches forward or back of that central point."

Bob then demonstrated how adding weight to the front or back of the model made it necessary to move the cord to different support hooks in order to keep the plane level.

"Single pilot, passengers, luggage, all move the CG and we don't want the plane to be too heavy in the nose or tail."

Bob held the plane so everyone could see the hooks sandwiched between two red lines. "As long as the center of gravity falls between the two lines, the plane is safe to fly. We'll produce a chart that will stay with the plane, giving different weight configurations and corresponding CG locations for a pilot to reference before a flight. The papers I just handed out explain all of this in more detail."

After recording the weight indicated on each scale, students huddled together filling out forms and making calculations. Once the group was satisfied, the team leader reported that the plane weighed seven hundred and fifty pounds and the center of gravity was right where it should be. After double-checking, it was made official. The plane was now registered, weighed, and ready for inspection.

The student inspection committee took over, removing the engine cowl, seats, and inspection plates. The team, equipped with flashlights and mirrors, gave the plane one last inspection, for after lunch, the DAR, or FAA Designated Airworthiness Representative, would inspect the plane and issue its airworthiness certificate.

Kate, who was not involved, was still very interested in the proceedings. After all, her uncle was going to own the RANS, and she was going to fly it after the break-in period.

After lunch, the EAA support team and DAR inspector began their work. Once they found the paperwork to be in order, they inspected each system in the aircraft—lubrication, cooling, electrical, exhaust, and airframe. There was one item, or squawk, that needed attending to, as two bolts were not safety-wired to the inspectors' liking and had to be redone, but in the end, the RANS S-7 Courier, built by the students at Center Valley High School, received its special airworthiness certificate and was ready to take to the air.

That evening, a dinner was given by the PTO in the school gymnasium for the entire school, complete with a photographer to take pictures of students sitting in the plane, headsets and all. Even the local news got into the excitement of the day, airing a story on the 10:00 news.

Chapter 21:
Dreams Take Flight

The sun had just poked above the horizon as hangar doors at Flabob Airport in Riverside, California, began opening.

Members of EAA Chapter 1 had work to do, for they were expecting a crowd to witness the first flight of Center Valley High School's Build-A-Plane project.

By the time parents and students started arriving, chapter members had pancakes, eggs, and bacon on the grill, and the RANS S-7 (which had had its wings removed then reinstalled at the airport) sitting in front of the hangar, awaiting its big day.

The airport, one of the oldest in the state, and a mecca for homebuilders and antique aircraft, had the reputation of being a shining example of how aviation could be a stimulus for education.

Kate got a ride to the airport with Jess, her mother, and Jess's new stepfather. Once there, she found Mr. Rice in casual dress walking with his wife and kids. Kate made it a point of introducing herself to Connie Rice and the children after saying hello.

"Big day, Kate!" Mr. Rice greeted.

"Big day, Mr. Rice!" she returned.

At the appointed time, Carl Terry, the chapter's resident instructor and the day's test pilot, gave the S-7 a thorough preflight.

Kate watched every move the test pilot made as he performed his preflight, committing them to memory, still amazed that she was looking at the aircraft she would be flying.

Carl informed the crowd that today's flight would be one hour long, and consist of simply taking off, climbing to four thousand feet, and circling the area, before landing and inspecting the engine. He explained that in all, forty hours of phase one testing would be required, with each flight exploring different aspects of flight while keeping careful records of performance.

Once inside and strapped in, Carl closed the door, checked side to side, yelled "Clear!" and started the engine. The students clapped and snapped pictures and videos as the plane began moving along the taxiway. The chapter had a loudspeaker set up so everyone could hear Carl's radio transmissions.

Finally the speakers came to life. "Flabob traffic, experimental one three three Charlie Victor taking runway two four for directional and brake evaluation, Flabob."

The aircraft rolled onto the runway, then accelerated and slowed several times. Reaching the far end, the craft repeated the process in the opposite direction.

Satisfied that all was in order, and allowing the engine to reach operating temperature, Carl announced on the radio and lined up on the center line.

Kate held her breath as the tail came up for a brief moment before going down as the plane lifted off in one smooth motion, climbing past the waving crowd into the

214

cool morning air. "Flabob traffic, one three three Charlie Victor turning crosswind, oil pressure holding, cylinder temps coming up. She feels real good."

Everyone watched as the tiny plane climbed higher and higher, making wide orbits around the airport. Every so often Carl reported temps and pressures. Kate and Jess watched as the craft climbed out of sight, lost against the cloudless sky. Finally giving up, Jess went over to talk with the other students, while Kate, finding a bench in the shade, sat quietly, contemplating the adventure that awaited her.

Lost in her thoughts Kate missed a call on the radio, but did hear Mr. Rice calling her over to the other students.

Kate stopped and looked up before running over to the crowd.

"Kate, he's only a few miles away, we wanted everyone together for Carl's arrival."

"Thanks, Mr. Rice, I was kind of lost in thought."

The speaker barked to life as Carl called his downwind and base leg.

"There he is!" one student shouted, pointing to the RANS as it prepared to turn final.

Some of the students began to cheer, but Kate stood motionless, watching every twitch her plane made as it approached its maiden landing. It was all so surreal!

The small plane touched down without a peep to the applause of everyone, and triumphantly taxied to a stop in front of the cheering students.

Carl dismounted and spoke with Bob McDonnell for

a moment then turned toward the hushed crowd. Smiling and still holding his clipboard, Carl looked at the students and said, "Well, you did it. You built a magnificent flying machine, and in doing so now belong to a very small and exclusive portion of the population. Congratulations! EAA Chapter 1 is very proud of you all!"

Following congratulations from their teachers and parents, the students presented Mr. Rice with a new aviation headset in appreciation of his hard work, then all posed for a group picture. After the RANS was moved off to the side, a Young Eagles rally got underway. Volunteer pilots using their own planes made sure that every student was given the opportunity to take a flight, and by the end of the day, twenty-one students had their Young Eagle logbooks and certificates.

Kate talked with Carl Terry for almost an hour, asking questions about the S-7 and the Rotax engine. Carl had nothing but praise and assured her that her uncle had made a wise investment.

As the day drew to a close, Mr. Rice walked over to Kate. "I wanted to thank you for reigniting my passion for flying." He stopped and looked over to the RANS. "Look at that plane, and think of all the knowledge everyone gained building it."

Kate smiled. "Mr. Rice, you did all the work. I'm glad Jess remembered you mentioning that you're a pilot."

Mr. Rice smiled. "Me too. Well, again, thank you, I'll see you in class Monday."

The school year came to an end a week later, with Jess starting her summer job at her stepfather's office, and

Kate off to Napa to complete her pilot training while continuing to help at the vineyard.

#

Kate added power to the tractor wheels as she headed back to the house. So many thoughts swirled through her head as she guided the big machine up the hill. She was now a high school senior, Bruce was working at home after his first year in college, and her flying lessons in the Cessna were going well. And today Jake was flying the RANS up to Clearview from Flabob. Phase one testing was complete, and her uncle Frank was now the owner of an airplane, of all things! And she was soon to be flying it to AirVenture.

Frank heard the tractor approaching and went outside, car keys in hand.

"How'd it go, Kate?" he asked as his niece made her now-customary dismount.

"Great, Uncle Frank. I didn't see any groundhogs today."

"Great. Why don't you get cleaned up, and you can drive me over to the airport to see my new airplane."

"I still can't believe you did this."

"Well, I understand it to be a good investment. Airplanes usually appreciate in value, so it will be easy to sell when the time comes."

"Who knows, maybe I'll want to buy it from you." Kate grinned before she hurried into the house.

"Who knows, maybe I'll take flying lessons, myself," Frank replied.

The two had just arrived at the airport when

Michelle met them at the door. "You guys are just in time. Jake called me an hour out, he needed a fuel stop and should be arriving any time now."

Almost as if on cue, the sound of an aircraft approached.

"There," Frank said, pointing to the south. In the sky, the RANS could be seen entering downwind, its bright yellow easy to spot from miles away. The trio watched as Jake made a perfect landing and taxied over to the office.

"Hey, Michelle, should I park here, or is the hangar ready for its new tenant?"

"Yep, hangar's ready. Here are two sets of keys for it," Michelle said, handing them to Frank.

"Thanks, Michelle. Here you go, Jake, and remember she's yours to fly whenever you like."

"Great—thanks. Tomorrow Kate and I are going to get familiar with this new plane. You're really going to get a kick flying her, Kate." Jake put the hangar key in his pocket and handed Kate the paper bag he was carrying.

Kate, with a puzzled look on her face, reached into the bag. "A fishing vest?" She studied it for a moment. "It's the same one you have on." Kate held up the short vest, festooned with pockets. "What's this for?"

"Well, missy, this tandem airplane doesn't give you many places to store things like pens, pads, batteries, earplugs, gum, tissues, sunglasses—you get the picture. This fishing vest is perfect for everything you need to have within reach as you fly. That one is yours. I even had it embroidered"

Kate smiled as she read the name "Missy."

218

"Yep," Jake said, smiling. "Thought of the name all by myself. Do you like it? You're gonna need it where we're going."

"Thanks, Jake," Kate said, putting on the vest. "Does it come with a fishing pole?"

Frank walked over and shook Jake's hand. "Thanks for going down and picking her up for me."

"Hey, listen, any time a guy gets to fly a new airplane for free, well, sign me up," Jake answered, winking at Frank as he opened the doors to let everyone get a good look. Then Frank hopped into the back seat for the short taxi over to the new hangar. Once the plane was put away, Frank treated everyone to lunch, with Sue and Chris joining them at the diner.

Kate could not contain her excitement after getting in the S-7. It had taken the better part of the morning for Jake to go over everything with her. Now it was time to fly.

"All right, missy, I'm all set back here. She flies like a sports car, so let's lift her off nice and easy, climb out at sixty-five, and we'll head for the practice area."

Kate guided the Courier onto the runway. "Clearview traffic, yellow/white high-wing Charlie Victor departing runway one eastbound, Clearview."

Kate pushed the throttle forward, adding right rudder.

"Whoa!" was all she could get out, overcontrolling for a moment as the plane accelerated, surprised at how responsive the rudder was.

A quick jab of left rudder and she was back over the center line as the tail came up. Kate added back pressure on the stick and they were up and away.

"Nice recovery, Kate," was the only comment from the rear.

Kate felt like a kid on Christmas morning with a new bike. The nimble S-7 had great visibility, and the tinted Lexan above her head allowed Kate to see where she was going during a steep turn by looking out through the top of the cockpit.

It took a while to get used to the flap handle and fuel gauge location, but only minutes for Kate to fall in love with how the new plane flew.

After landing, Jake signed Kate off in her logbook as being qualified to fly the S-7 and had her fly the new plane by herself for another hour, before putting it away for the night.

Chapter 22:
Anticipation

By the third week of July, Kate had logged twelve hours solo in her uncle's plane and was well into planning the trip from Napa to Wittman Field in Oshkosh, Wisconsin.

Fuel stops, airspace considerations, including Military Operations Areas, or MOAs, and restricted airspace had been worked out. That evening, Kate sat at the kitchen table memorizing the AirVenture arrival procedure when Frank came in and sat next to her.

"How's it going, Kate?"

"All right, Uncle Frank. I'm just going over what I have to do when I get close to Wittman Field."

"I remember you telling me that it's like a military maneuver or something. Why don't you explain it to me?"

Kate smiled, recognizing an opportunity to reinforce what she had learned.

"As we approach Oshkosh, I have to fly at one hundred four miles per hour toward the town of Ripon at an altitude of eighteen hundred feet. Over the town, I fall in single file and a half mile behind other aircraft as we follow the railroad tracks toward the town of Fisk. That's the part that worries me; I just hope the sky isn't too crowded."

"So the picture you were studying as I walked in is the railroad tracks from the air."

"Yes, and you can see the road running parallel, and look at this bend in the road. Anyway, as we reach the town of Fisk, air traffic controllers on the ground will identify me and have me rock my wings, as verification that they're talking to the right plane."

"Can't you just talk to them?" Frank asked.

"No, too many planes. We just listen. So after I rock my wings, Fisk controllers will tell me to either turn east to land on runway three six/one eight or continue following the tracks for a landing on runway two seven/zero niner. After that I switch to the tower frequency. They tell me when to turn final and which colored dot to land on."

Frank thought a moment. "What's up with the dots?"

Kate laughed. "They have huge colored dots painted on the runway thousands of feet apart, so small planes can land and exit the same runway simultaneously."

"That sounds like a lot of fun, Kate. You have that down pat. I'm sure you're going to do great." With that vote of confidence, Frank gave Kate a kiss on the forehead and turned in for the night.

Saturday morning brought low clouds and mist to Napa Valley, something very unusual for this time of year. However, Kate never noticed, for today she would be packing for Oshkosh, and finalizing arrangements for her and Jake's two overnights. The S-7 could hold fifty pounds maximum in the luggage compartment located behind the rear seat. Jake figured they could each bring fifteen pounds of baggage and still have room for the tie-down kit, oil, some tools, and other essential items. Kate weighed everything and was happy to see that she was underweight by one pound.

The plan called for the flight to make its first fuel stop in Derby Field (LOL) in Nevada more than two hundred miles away, then continue over the salt flats to Ogden, Utah. There she and Jake would spend the night with Jake's friend Donny Doyle and his family. From Ogden, the pair would fly to Converse County Airport (DWG) in Wyoming some three hundred miles away, fuel up, and continue on to Marv Skie Airport (Y14) in Sioux Falls, South Dakota. There they would stay with her mother's cousin Linda Hays and her husband, Peter.

The big day would be an early one. If all went well, the pair would blast off at 6:00 a.m. and fly three hundred thirty-five miles to Mauston/New Lisbon Union Airport (82C) just sixty-nine miles from Oshkosh, refuel, and shoot the arrival procedure into AirVenture at approximately 10:00 a.m.

Her mom and dad would meet them there, having arrived the evening before, and her schoolmates would meet up with them by noon the same day.

Now all she had to do was to *do it!*

Lake Valley reservoir gleamed in the sunlight fifteen hundred feet beneath the RANS S-7. Kate was wearing her vest and hat, its brim sitting low on her forehead, just above her new sunglasses as she flew into the morning sun. Kate and Jake had taken off at 7:00 a.m. and were well on their way to their first fuel stop in

Nevada.

Kate had decided to intercept highway I-80 near the Sierra Nevada foothills and follow it as it wound its way east through the mountains. Besides not having to climb over the high peaks, the interstate provided a great place to land in case of emergency.

As they approached the interstate, Kate checked the Garmin 296 portable GPS unit in the center of the instrument panel that Jake had mounted to help navigate around complicated airspace, and for the arrival into Wittman Field. Even with the sun in her eyes, Kate was in awe of the mountains that lay before her as she turned east over the highway, for today was a day of firsts, and she was determined not to take a single moment for granted. As they climbed, Jake pointed out Donner Pass, where the ill-fated wagon train was stranded by snow. Kate looked up at the mountaintops towering a thousand feet above them. Even though her altimeter read seven thousand nine hundred, she was only seven hundred feet above I-80.

"So Kate, I'll bet you're happy about your decision to follow the highway over the mountains."

"How do you do that? I'm thinking it and you say it. Gosh, we're so high and yet so close to the ground. This airplane is feeling smaller and smaller."

Jake chuckled to himself. "I know, these mountains make everyone feel small, and I'm certainly not a mind reader. I just know what you're feeling because everyone feels the same way the first time. And we have a great day to do this, not much wind. These little planes have their limitations, just make sure you don't ask it to do more than it was designed to do."

"I won't, Jake, this is some serious shi...stuff."

Jake laughed.

Things got busy as Kate contacted Reno Approach Control to transit through their airspace. Once clear of Reno, and the mountains behind her, Kate had time to appreciate the endless dry lake beds spreading out in front of her. She could only imagine the dread early pioneers felt as the mountains grew out of the horizon ahead of their wagon trains.

A blast of heat greeted Kate as she descended toward her first fuel stop. Already sweating, she taxied up to the self-service fuel pumps, surprised to find two planes waiting as a third pilot finished fueling up.

Jake talked with the other pilots while Kate visited the pilot's lounge, surprised to find another woman waiting to use the facilities. Kate figured that the woman was in her sixties, with short brown hair and a lot of makeup.

"Oh honey, come in and get out of the heat, sweetheart. Where are you from? No, let me guess. Listen, young lady, you need to put your hair up, it's way too hot to have it down. I mean, it's beautiful, but here, let me fix you up."

Kate never got a word in as the woman went into her bag for a rubber band, spun Kate around, and put her hair up in a ponytail.

"There you go, dolly, now you're all set for the heat. Here, give me your hat."

Kate walked out of the pilot's lounge still trying to figure out what had happened. Back at the plane, Jake said, "Good news, kiddo. Winds aloft are stronger than forecast. We're going to have a thirty-mile-an-hour tailwind today and tomorrow. Our ground speed will be one forty!"

"Wow!"

"I already called my buddy, Don," Jake continued, "and let him know we'll be arriving early. His wife Sally will pick us up. Uh...what happened to your hair?"

Kate's new ponytail was sticking out from her hat. She shrugged. "I think the heat is getting to people."

Jake laughed. "Don't let the locals hear you say that. They like it here."

Kate was happy to get back to altitude as nature's air conditioning cooled things off. However, navigation wasn't going to be easy on this leg, as Jake had decided to turn the GPS off, and challenged Kate to fly to Ogden using chart and compass only.

It wasn't as hard as it seemed, though. Kate had studied the maps and charts, and knew each mountain range. Besides, I-80 ran parallel to their course, allowing Kate to use it as a handrail. As long as she could see the highway off to her right, she couldn't be far off course.

With the tailwind pushing her east, Kate reached the edge of the Great Salt Lake only a half hour after refueling. Its white salt flats stretched for miles. She was happy that the sun was now behind them, as the glare from the morning sun would have made her next navigation challenge difficult. To avoid a restricted area that their course ran through, Kate would have to fly north around two sets of mountains and find the east–west train tracks on the northern border of the restricted airspace. Kate would have to keep the tracks off to her right and follow them into Ogden.

"I see the tracks," Kate announced as the small plane came around the north side of the mountain.

"Good going, missy," Jake answered, proud of his student. "Now remember your altitudes as we get across the lake and make sure you have your radio set up."

Kate repeated the instructions and dialed in the automated terminal information and tower frequency before checking the airport diagram.

The landing went without a hitch, and after refueling and tying down, Jake introduced Kate to his friend Donny's wife, Sally. That evening, Kate was entertained by stories from the past, and she enjoyed watching the two men poke good-natured fun at each other.

The two aviators were up early the next day and blasted off into the cool morning air on the first leg of a seven-hundred-mile day. Again the tailwind gods smiled on the small plane by providing another thirty-mile-per-hour west wind. Cruising along at one hundred forty, Jake decided to fly past their planned fuel stop and land forty-nine miles further, landing at a nicer airport. "Don't get too used to these ground speeds, Kate. It's rare that things line up like this. You can bet we'll pay for it on the way back," Jake said with a touch of cynicism in his voice.

The second and longest leg was cut down to one

hour and forty minutes, allowing the S-7 to touch down in Sioux Falls, South Dakota, a full hour early. Kate was happy to see her mother's cousin Linda and her husband, Peter. Peter taught math at the local high school and was very interested in the Build-A-Plane Program, and Kate's flying adventures, and had arranged for several students and the school's principal to see the S-7, and speak with her about Build-A-Plane. Kate felt like a celebrity as she fielded questions and posed for pictures. After dinner, Jake and Kate planned the next day's flight into AirVenture. They planned to be in the air by 6:00 a.m. and fly some three hundred miles to Mauston Airport in Wisconsin, top off the fuel tanks, and rest. Then a quick eighty miles to Ripon, where Kate would fall in behind other aircraft forming a single line of planes, and fly the approach procedure.

"What's the plan if we get to Ripon and it's loaded with airplanes?" Kate asked, doing her best to hide her anxiety.

"That's why we're going in with full tanks, Kate. Risk mitigation. It's amazing how one minute the sky is thick with airplanes and five minutes later there's not a plane to be seen, for a few minutes, anyway. We can always find a nice farm a few miles away, drop down to seven hundred feet, and just orbit for a few minutes until things calm down."

That made sense to Kate, and she spent the remainder of the evening talking with her cousins, and talking on the phone with her mother, whose scheduled flight landed in Oshkosh that afternoon.

228

Chapter 23:
Welcome to Oshkosh!

The sun was just coming up as Kate finished loading bags into the rear baggage compartment and Jake and Peter arrived with breakfast sandwiches.

Kate felt jittery as she ate. One part of her couldn't wait to take off, while the other part wished the day was already over.

After finishing up, Kate said her good-byes and strapped in, as ready as she would ever be.

Again the plane containing the two aviators performed great in the cool morning air, taking advantage of the fifteen-mile-an-hour tailwind, shaving thirty minutes off the flight from Sioux Falls to Mauston Airport. Now the RANS was fueled and ready for the final leg of this fantastic fifteen-hundred-mile journey of a lifetime. The final eighty miles would be spent monitoring the radio and getting a feel for what type of traffic the pair should expect.

Kate's stomach tightened as she prepared to strap in.

"Look, missy, just remember your training and try not to let anything rattle you. I figure we only have so much brainpower; let's not waste any of it on worry. Other than that, it's all you today, but remember I have your back."

Kate smiled. "I'm all set, Jake. Let's do this!"

Kate put her right hand on the key, knowing that her next shutdown would be in Oshkosh!

She advanced the S-7's throttle, instinctively feeding in just enough right rudder as the tail came up.

Kate felt a heightened state of awareness as she climbed into the sky, listening to the sound of the engine, feeling the chill of the morning air, and enjoying the responsiveness of the S-7, something that would prove important a short time later. The landscape ahead was beautiful, its rich green fields dotted with barns, silos, and tree-lined creeks glistening in the sun. A welcome sight, in stark contrast to the barren landscape of yesterday.

"Okay, kiddo, time to turn the transponder off. Now we'll be just another small dot, all headed for the same place. So many transponders in one small area would turn ATC radar screens solid white."

Kate reached forward and turned off the transponder, then turned up the radio volume, causing a chill to run through her as she listened to the unbroken staccato of rapid-fire radio instructions from Fisk Control.

"All right, everybody out there. I see a lot of planes approaching from Ripon—it looks like you're all spread out, you need to be in a single file directly over the railroad tracks. If the tracks are out your left or right window, you're not over them. You need to be looking at them at twelve o'clock, eighteen hundred feet, and ninety knots. Okay, Cessna 150 approaching Fisk, rock your wings. Cessna 150, follow the tracks in front to the gravel pit and turn downwind for two seven, monitor the tower on one one eight point five. The red Champ, rock your wings. Red

Champ, thank you, make a right turn now, right turn now, fly eastbound and follow the east–west road. Make left traffic for runway three six, monitor one two six point six. Okay, there's a 150 with the wig-wag lights approaching Fisk, if you hear me rock your wings. Okay, good rock, wig-wag, follow the tracks to the gravel pit for right traffic runway two seven. I need half-mile spacing from the plane in front of you, monitor one one eight point five. Okay, there's a low-wing, looks like he's a little high, rock your wings. Okay, start a right turn—sir, I don't see your gear, you have to get the gear down and start slowing down. You're following a red Champ off your right side on base leg for runway three six, monitor tower on one two six point six…"

Jake broke Kate's trance, his voice calm and confident. "Okay, missy, this doesn't sound too bad, and it's only going to get worse as time goes on, so we're going straight in, we're about seven miles out. Remember, you're scanning for traffic in front and on your left. I'll help with traffic in front and on the right. Okay, eighteen hundred feet and one hundred four. Stay sharp, kid, here we go."

Kate had her marching orders. Her stomach was tight as she scanned the sky ahead. "Ten o'clock, about one-and-a-half miles, moving in the same direction, and another at nine, a bit closer."

"That's okay, Kate, just keep an eye on them. We're all going to Ripon, that's it up ahead."

Kate's heart began to race, her grip tightening on the stick, as she saw the homes, buildings, and water tower coming into view. *This is it!*

For a moment, Kate wanted to turn away, yet knew she had to push on, like the day she soloed. She needed to do this.

"All right, Kate, I have traffic at two o'clock and one at four o'clock. Ripon is four miles ahead. Oh, and stop squeezing the stick so tight."

How does he do that? Kate thought as she loosened her grip on the stick.

"I know everything, remember," Jake reminded her. "It looks to me like the planes on your side have a better angle, and I think we're coming in a bit south of where the railroad tracks are." He waited to hear Kate's plan.

"Let's slide over to the north and fall in behind the two planes on my side," Kate replied, seeing that her targets were on more of a straight line into the center of town. "This might be the beginning of the conga line."

Laser-focused on the task at hand, Kate maneuvered to the left, as if the plane was part of her, her thoughts conveyed telepathically.

"Nice job, missy. My targets got the message, and I think they might be coming in behind us."

Five planes were falling in line as they reached Ripon, like a well-rehearsed aerial ballet. Kate was number three behind a blue low-wing with black wingtips. *This is amazing!* she thought, as she fell in behind the two aircraft to her front, knowing that other aircraft were falling in line behind her. Kate felt...no, she knew she was part of something *big*, something *special!*

Now the landscape Kate had memorized in the arrival NOTAM spread out before her as if she had been there before.

Suddenly an object appeared on her side! Kate flinched as out of nowhere a large plane passed off to her left, moving much faster, pulled up, and was gone.

"Whoa, did you see that!" she yelled, her momentary fright causing the plane to jump.

But Jake was scanning the sky to his right. "I didn't see anything, Kate. Fly the plane. We're into it."

Kate took a deep breath and steadied herself as she again scanned for traffic, and focused on listening to the controllers giving unbroken rapid-fire instructions.

"Okay, red and white Citabria, rock your wings. Good rock, sir, start a right turn and follow the east–west road, monitor tower on one two six point six for left traffic, runway three six." The controller paused for a moment. "I see several planes coming up from Ripon, remember eighteen hundred feet and ninety knots, folks, and I need half-mile spacing. You have to be over the tracks, not off to the side. Let's go, number three—you're not over the tracks."

"Oh no, that's me, Jake. I drifted!"

"I'm done talking, kiddo. Unless you do something unsafe, it's all you, so pay attention and give him a good rock when he tells you."

"That's it, number three, nice job moving over. Cessna approaching Fisk, keep your speed up, and you look to be low. Eighteen hundred feet, please, you have four behind you."

Kate had never experienced such tension or level of concentration; her heart was pounding so hard she could barely breathe!

"Okay, white Cessna over Fisk, rock your wings. Cessna, rock your wings. Good rock, turn right now, Cessna, turn right and follow the east–west road, switch to tower one two six point six, left traffic for three six. Blue RV with black tips, rock your wings. RV, I can't tell if you're rocking your wings, sir. There you go, good rock, follow the tracks to the gravel pit and monitor one one eight point five, right traffic into runway two seven. Yellow/white RANS, approaching Fisk—"

"Oh God, that's me!" Kate held her breath.

"Rock your wings."

Kate threw the stick full left, causing the left wing to drop, then full over to the right. The plane banked so sharply left, right, and left that the controllers on the ground could be heard chuckling as the lead controller continued, "Best rock we've seen all day, RANS, good job. Right turn now, RANS, right turn, follow the white Cessna and monitor one two six point six, twenty-six-six for left traffic into three six. White 172 approaching Fisk, rock your wings..."

Kate banked to the right, knowing exactly where she was. In the distance she saw Lake Winnebago, and off to her eleven o'clock, Wittman Field, Oshkosh! Kate tried to shake off the tension and returned to keeping her eye on the Cessna in front of her as she dialed in one two six point six and hit the Select button.

A different voice came over the radio, a woman's,

calm, reassuring, giving instructions to the endless line of arriving aircraft. "Red/white Citabria, stop your descent and hold your speed all the way in, sir. You can land at the orange dot, the orange dot for the red/white Citabria, cleared to land three six, then make a left onto the grass, great job everybody. Cessna, turn final now, Cessna turn final. White Cessna 150 on base, I'm talking to you, turn final now, please!"

Kate sensed that the Cessna in front of her might be having an issue, but she remained focused on airspeed, spacing, and traffic scan as the plane to her front finally turned final.

She glanced to her left and saw thousands of people stretched out along the side of the taxiway watching planes land. "Holy mackerel, look at the crowd!" Kate blurted.

"Never mind that, missy, get ready to turn final and keep an eye on the plane in front, sounds like he's spooked," Jake said.

"Cessna on final for three six, I need you on the yellow dot, keep it coming all the way to the yellow dot. Yellow/white RANS on base, you can turn final now, turn final and start descending."

Kate made the turn from base to final. It was almost over! But as she turned, she saw that the plane in front of her was too low and slow to make it to the yellow dot if they didn't add power, and she felt the distance between them shrinking.

The controller saw it, too, but didn't want to rattle the Cessna pilot and make a bad situation worse. "Cessna, that's okay, Cessna, you're doing great, you can land short of the yellow dot and move onto the grass. Yellow/white RANS, I need you to land well short of the first dot, put it on the numbers for me, yellow/white, or I'll have to take you around. Mooney on base, turn final and do not descend."

Kate reacted instinctively, pulling back the throttle and pulling the stick to the left, dropping the left wing as she kicked in full right rudder to force the S-7 into a deep slip. Down they went like a runaway elevator, putting Kate's short-field training and the S-7's agility to the test.

"That's it, kid, show her what you got," Jake encouraged. "Be ready with some power."

"Great slip, yellow/white, on the numbers for me and off onto the grass."

Kate held the slip right down to the ground, raised the nose to arrest the descent and burn off excess speed, before kicking out the slip, and adding a brief bit of power as she flared...touchdown! Power to idle! Retract flaps! Pull the stick into your belly and apply the brakes, keeping it straight and slowing down. Now roll past the lights and off onto the grass, just past the numbers.

"Welcome to Oshkosh, yellow/white. Thanks for helping out! Okay, Mooney, clear to land blue dot, you can keep your speed up, blue dot and you can taxi to the end of the runway..."

Kate was stunned. She'd done it all without thinking. She was the plane!

"Nicely done, missy. Let's get away from all this movement as soon as possible."

236

Kate's stomach was so tight it hurt, but kept the plane moving as successive linemen waved her forward, making her feel as if she was on a huge conveyor belt of airplanes. Jake leaned forward and handed Kate an eight-by-eleven-inch paper sign. "Put this '301' sign in the windshield. The linemen will see it and guide us to row 301, that's where the RANS people are parking."

Focused on following taxi instructions and not hitting anything, Kate never noticed the throngs of people watching as she navigated along the taxiway behind the other aircraft until finally being instructed to turn into the line of parked RANS airplanes. Kate taxied slowly through the grass up to an open spot, stopped, and shut down, almost refusing to believe that she had actually pulled it off, as exhaustion and elation swept over her.

"You did it all on your own there, Kate. I'm proud of you!"

Jake's words opened the floodgates as tears of happiness burst out of Kate's eyes as she laughed and cried at the same time.

"That's okay, kid, let it out. It's a lot of tension, just let it out," the big man encouraged in an understanding tone. He waited a moment, then reached forward and opened the door.

"Okay, enough of that. People are looking at you and we have work to do."

Kate turned back and looked at him through her tears as she laughed. "What happened to just let it out?"

"Yeah, well, that was before I saw your parents walking this way."

Kate stopped crying and laughed, shaking her head as she unbuckled and climbed out. The entire nerve-racking episode from Ripon to Fisk to touchdown had taken less than fifteen minutes, minutes that Kate would never forget.

As her parents approached, Anna, seeing what looked like tears in her daughter's eyes, hugged her as her father patted her back and asked, "How was it, honey? Was it as difficult as you thought?"

Kate looked at Jake, then at her father. "Nope, it was a piece of cake, Dad." Bob looked at Jake, who nodded and said, "Yep, and she handled it all by herself, I was just along for the ride."

After tying down the RANS, Jake called Chris to see where she and the school students were.

Chris, along with Mr. Rice and several parents, had volunteered to chaperone the school trip and arranged to meet everyone in front of the control tower, where Kate joined the other students, allowing her parents, aunt, and uncle to go off in another direction.

Even as they walked, the students had a hard time grasping the immensity of the event. There were thousands of planes of every shape, size, and category.

In the center of the display area called Boeing Plaza, vintage airliners shared space with jet fighters past and present, along with a U-2 spy plane and Sea King helicopter. Thousands of tents and RVs filled the numerous campgrounds, and to the north, people camped right next to their aircraft in the area known as the North Forty. To the west, large pavilions were jammed with vendors displaying the latest in services, aircraft accessories, and electronics.

The students loved visiting the huge white tent showrooms, complete with air conditioning, sod lawns, and landscaping, showing off the latest in personal jets and aircraft.

It was already dark when Kate and her family arrived at a restaurant for dinner. "Mom, why are we sitting at such a large table? I thought Jake and Chris were having dinner with friends." Before Anna could answer, Kate noticed her dad, smiling and standing up. Kate looked at the door and saw Bruce!

Bruce was here, with his family! Kate shot up and ran into his arms. "I can't believe you're here! I'm so happy!"

As they took their seats, Sue and Frank moved over so Bruce and Kate could sit next to each other.

The next day, Kate dragged Bruce around the show grounds all day, explaining this and that, then they sat hand in hand watching the air show as world-famous aerial acts and vintage piston fighter formations filled the sky.

The highlight of the afternoon was seeing the school's RANS S-7 take part in Homebuilts in Review. After attending a pilot briefing, Jake joined several other pilots in hand-picked homebuilts, flying one after another only two hundred feet above the ground along the length of the runway, passing in front of thousands, as an announcer read each plane's bio over the loudspeaker system. It was a thrill for Mr. Rice and the students to listen to the crowd cheer after hearing that the beautiful yellow/white RANS S-7 was built by high school students.

After the homebuilt review, Bruce and Kate split up from the others to walk around by themselves.

"What do you think?" Kate asked him. "Are you having a good time?"

Bruce looked at her and smiled. "It's amazing. I still can't believe it. Is it what you expected?"

Kate looked around. "I never expected it to be this big. I can't believe I flew in."

"I can't believe it, either, but Kate—you did it!"

Bruce stopped and took something out of his pocket. "Kate, this is my 4-H pin. It means a lot to me. I'd like you to have it."

Kate looked at the pin and then at Bruce, smiling. "You're asking me to go steady?"

Bruce chuckled. "Yes, silly, but no one calls it that anymore. Don't lose it."

The two kissed, right in front of the famous F-4 Phantom jet fighter. "I'll take that as a yes," Bruce said, holding Kate's hand that much tighter.

"Okay, you two, what's going on?" Bruce's mom, Laura, asked as the four parents met them for dinner. "Too much smiling going on here."

Kate displayed the 4-H pin that Bruce had pinned to her blouse. "Bruce asked me to go steady."

Everyone smiled, Bob shook Bruce's hand and gave Kate a big hug, as did Bruce's mom and dad, and Anna kissed and hugged everybody! Later that evening, Jake and Chris, who had met up with everyone for dinner, ordered the young couple a bottle of champagne, which got a huge laugh seeing as they were at a Denny's.

The highlight of day three, everyone's final day, was spent at seminars, the homebuilt area, and the One Week Wonder pavilion, where volunteers were building a Zenith 701 kit in only one week. People waited in line for the privilege of working on the plane, some installing a single rivet. The plane would fly on the last day of AirVenture.

That evening, Kate and Jake got together with her parents to discuss their departure plans for the next morning. It would be an early start in an effort to get ahead of the rush and depart ahead of any convective buildup.

Later that night, after saying good night to her parents, Kate got into bed and stared up at the ceiling, revisiting the events of the past week. Closing her eyes, she could see the mountain peaks passing by as she navigated Donner Pass, and the stark beauty of the salt flats. She relived every moment from Ripon to touchdown and smiled as her thoughts turned to Bruce asking her to wear his pin. Turning over, Kate fell into a deep sleep.

Chapter 24:
Moving On

Kate and her father were lucky to arrive at the tie-down area on time the next morning, after hitching a ride with two pilots staying at their hotel.

As she and her father neared row 301, she saw that Jake had already enlisted the help of some early risers to pull the S-7 past the show line and up to the taxiway. "Good morning, missy, good morning, Bob," Jake said as he finished putting his things in the plane.

"Good morning, Mr. Jake," Kate answered with a smile.

"Back to that again, I see," Jake said with a chuckle.

"You were here early," Bob said as the two men shook hands.

"Yeah, I had a lot of things to sort through before the flight. Looks good, Kate. Headwinds are forecast to be light for the next three days. I think we might get a break."

"That sounds great, Jake. All I could think about on the way over here was the prospect of a seventy-mile-an-hour ground speed. I just spoke with Flight Service and got the same info—light winds, good visibility, and no weather in the direction of flight."

"Good work, missy, glad to see some of the stuff I taught you is sinking in. Let's get this plane loaded and moving before the rush."

"I have water bottles for us and some granola

bars," Kate offered as she put on her fishing vest.

After the preflight and buckling up, the S-7 roared to life and sat idling as Kate made sure everything was in order.

"All right, missy, contact ground and let them know we're VFR and ready to taxi to the active."

Kate paused for a moment as she took everything in. The early-morning chill, rows and rows of aircraft, and the wonderful man sitting behind her. How lucky she was to have met him.

Chapter 25:
The Sands of Time

"Oshkosh Ground, Southwest fourteen thirty ready to taxi from the terminal with information Bravo."

"Roger, Southwest fourteen thirty, taxi alpha cross runway two seven, cross runway two three, to taxiway alpha one, hold short runway one eight, contact tower on one one eight point five."

First Officer Kate Gillman sitting in the right seat of the Southwest Boeing 737 read back the instructions. "Taxi alpha, cross two seven, cross two three, to alpha one, hold short runway one eight, contact tower one one eight point five."

ATC responded, "Southwest fourteen thirty, cleared to taxi."

Kate looked out from her lofty perch past the Boeing 737's right wing. "Clear on the right," the newly minted first officer told the captain.

The captain advanced the dual throttles, checking the engine gauges as the airliner started moving forward. Although the captain was taxiing the aircraft, it was First Officer Kate Gillman's leg to fly, and the fact that it was the leg from Oshkosh to Los Angeles was not lost on the now twenty-six-year-old first officer.

At the hold line to runway one eight, Kate switched over to the tower, and let them know that they were ready to go.

"Southwest fourteen thirty, hold for arriving 757, then line up and wait, runway one eight."

Kate read back her hold short instructions, then took a moment to look across the runway at the grass, where so many years ago she and Jake had begun their journey home. So many memories.

Kate watched the 757-fly past them, waiting to confirm its touchdown before the captain guided the airliner onto the runway center line. "Your aircraft to fly, Kate."

Kate smiled. "I have control."

"You have control."

"Southwest fourteen thirty cleared to take off."

"Clear to take off, fourteen thirty."

Kate set takeoff power and steered the large craft over the rapidly passing center lines until it reached the commitment speed for takeoff, at which point the captain announced, "Rotate."

Kate pulled smoothly on the yoke and established a fifteen-degree climb. "Positive rate," she announced. "Gear up."

The flight to Los Angeles was uneventful and very smooth. Not like the bumps Kate and Jake were forced to endure on the first day of their return trip from Oshkosh. Unlike the flight home in the RANS, however, Kate could not foresee what awaited her in the dispatch office after the flight.

"Kate!" the crew scheduling officer called as Kate walked into Southwest's briefing room in LAX. "We have a stand-in for your next leg to Phoenix. You have an urgent message from a Frank Wilson. You can call from the lounge."

Kate was shaken; something was wrong, and the airline had already found a replacement for her next flight. "Uncle Frank, it's Kate. What's wrong!"

A day later, Kate walked into church holding her husband's hand, entering the pew behind Chris Hollerman and other family members. All of the Wilsons joined Bruce and Kate as the newlyweds knelt to say a prayer.

Kate's dear friend and mentor Jake Hollerman had passed, after a six-month fight with lung cancer.

Over the years, Kate had spent many hours with Jake and Chris and talked with him often but was still shocked that her friend was gone.

At the appointed time, Frank walked up to the podium, paused for a moment, and then spoke.

"We come here today to remember, to honor, to say good-bye to a good man. A brave man who served his country, and gave freely of his time to friends and strangers alike. Jake Hollerman was much like the fictional men you see in movies—strong, quiet, and consistent in his convictions—except Jake was the real thing. He loved to fly and shared that love with many. He told me how lucky he was to meet his wife, Chris, and loved her dearly. He also told me how rewarding it felt to have the opportunity to share his love of flight with so many young people. Jake leaves behind a legacy of loyalty to family, friends, and country. He will be missed. The last time I saw Jake, he asked me to remind everyone to remember only the good times, and never take the small things for granted. Thank you, Jake, you're a good man."

Jake was buried with full military, honors, complete with a flyover by five Army Black Hawk helicopters in the missing man formation. Taps were played as the honor guard removed the American flag from the big man's coffin, folded it, and handed it to Jake's widow.

Afterward a luncheon was held at the diner, which had been closed out of respect for Jake by the owner. During the meal, Chris came over and sat next to the newlyweds. "Kate, before you and Bruce go back home to the vineyard, would you please follow me over to the airport? Jake wanted you to have something that he left for you in the hangar."

Kate felt transported back in time as she and Bruce walked with Chris from the airport parking lot along the road behind the hangars. As they turned the corner between the two hangars, Kate saw the open door of Jake's hangar. Walking forward she could see the nose of an airplane, the yellow airplane, exactly as she had seen it for the first time so many years ago, sitting just where Jake had left it, patiently waiting to grace the sky. Chris stopped at the hangar door. "Go ahead, Kate, it's on the desk."

Kate looked at Chris, and then Bruce, before walking in alone. There on the desk sat a framed picture of her and Jake standing in front of the S-7 at Oshkosh. The picture sat on a white envelope, which Kate picked up, removing the handwritten card.

Hi, missy,

Kate spun around, for she could have sworn she heard Jake's voice. Then she took a deep breath and, through her tears, began to read.

Hi, missy,

I need someone to take care of old Annabelle here, and I figure you're the one who will appreciate her the most. Chris is on board with this, so don't bother offering her anything, she won't take it. Remember, kid, you never really own a vintage airplane, you're just the caretaker for a while. Take care of her for me. And thank you. Teaching you to fly and watching you spread your wings was something I thought I would never get to experience after losing my daughter, Mary.

You brought me such joy. Now go on and get out of here, and stop crying, people are watching.

Jake

Epilogue

Kate's hair blew gently to the side as the Piper Cub flew gracefully over the rolling hills and vineyards that dotted the landscape. Kate banked the craft gracefully around the rising terrain, looking down at the ice cream parlor, and her uncle's vineyard, the tractor, parked in its usual spot. Sitting up front in her car seat, Kate's five-year-old daughter sat transfixed as the Cub approached three hot air balloons ascending into the crisp air. It was a perfect evening.

One with the sky, Kate again felt like that young girl of fifteen, savoring the moment, forever thankful to the man with the big heart who had given her the gift of flight.

About the Author

The author is a Private Pilot living near Allentown, Pennsylvania

Made in the USA
Las Vegas, NV
18 July 2023

74929806R00144